GRAY SLEEP

A Novel

By Dominic Vaiana

ALSO BY DOMINIC VAIANA

A Bar in Toledo: The Untold Story of a Mafia Front Man and a Grammy-Winning Song

ISBN 979-8-9989625-0-9

"He knew that he had no honor which the world could recognize. His life, passions, trials, loves, were, at worst, filth, and, at best, disease in the eyes of the world, and crimes in the eyes of his countrymen. There were no standards for him except those he could make for himself. There were no standards for him because he could not accept the definitions, the hideously mechanical jargon of the age. He saw no one around him worth his envy, did not believe in the vast, gray sleep which was called security, did not believe in the cures, panaceas, and slogans which afflicted the world he knew; and this meant that he had to create his standards and make up his definitions as he went along."

— James Baldwin

If it seems like I don't care
It doesn't mean I don't care
It just looks like I don't care
Because my emotions have been sanded off
I live in LA, sweetie, what do you expect?

— Thundercat & Tame Impala

"We are punished by our sins, not for them."

— Elbert Hubbard

Flirting with Lana at Pool

WHILE I TALK TO HER I'm flexing my abs so hard they start to cramp. It hurts, but this is what I need to do—or tell myself I need to do—to command her attention. Get her mind off the British scumbag who was massaging sunscreen on her back last weekend. The midday sun casts sharp, vertical shadows that accentuate the contours of my muscles, and even though I can't see her eyes behind her Bottega Veneta sunglasses, I know they're scanning my torso: the lean, symmetrical product of high-intensity weight training and a daily protein intake of 152 grams.

We're poolside at my residential tower just off Santa Monica, which is home to 277 young people with no shame and a lot of money to burn, including a rookie pitcher on the Dodgers, a rapper on *XXL* magazine's Freshman Class list, an heir to a Saudi oil empire who's in and out of rehab, a Chinese amusement park tycoon with a private security staff, and a college dropout who invented a chewing gum infused with the same active ingredient as Viagra.

Then there's me and Lana. We're recapping our spring vacations, so I mention the villa in Ibiza, making sure to pronounce it *eye-beeth-a*.

"Ibiza..." She cocks her head. "Doesn't Ibiza get a little *chilly* in March?"

Her phone buzzes on the table beside her—a Raya notification that disappears before I can read it.

"Did I say Ibiza?" I say, forcing a chuckle. "I meant *Tulum*."

I haven't been to Ibiza or Tulum since college and need to pivot fast, but I'm distracted by the show Lana's putting on for me: the sun-kissed skin glistening with a coat of tanning oil, the gentle flare of her hips from the narrow cinch of her waist, the swell of her breasts, barely contained by the red fabric of her triangle-cut Frankies bikini top—a masterclass in anatomical perfection.

On her left bicep, she has a small tattoo that reads "1998" between two small angel wings, and she has "BREATHE" tattooed horizontally across the inside of her right wrist. I usually hate tattoos on girls because they demonstrate poor impulse control, but I'm willing to make an exception for Lana: 24 years old, just broke up with some real estate scam artist, a Tri Delta sorority member who majored in communications at the University of Arizona (opened her legs more than she opened any books), freelance photographer (also known as unemployed), expensive taste in vintage fashion and natural wine—vain in all the fun ways. She may have a slight eating disorder. Her dad racked up an obscene fortune from film packaging during the 80s, which now covers Lana's apartment lease, Range Rover Velar payment, shoe collection, and Equinox global membership.

I play dumb and ask if her boyfriend is joining her at the pool soon.

"I'm actually single—by *choice*," she stresses.

"You don't carry yourself like a single woman," I say, knowing this will get her going.

"What's that supposed to mean?" she asks, second-guessing herself.

"You have 'fuck off' written across your forehead."

She brushes a lock of sand-brown hair behind her ear, arching one immaculately pedicured foot.

"I'm focusing on self-care this year," she says absently.

"Do you normally focus on care for others?" I ask, sipping Clase Azul out of an Acqua Panna bottle. "Hand out clothes on Skid Row? Volunteer at the soup kitchens?"

This gets a grin.

"You're an asshole."

"I've been called worse."

She giggles while taking a sip of something green from a paper straw. On the table beside her is a copy of *Do Nothing: How to Break Away from Overworking, Overdoing, and Underliving*. Based on the placement of her bookmark, she's barely past the table of contents.

"What's so interesting on your phone?" I ask, trying to ignore a drop of sunscreen-infused sweat burning my right eye. "Catching up on all the DMs from your reply guys?"

"If you *must* know, I've been looking at new art for my living room. The prints I bought when I moved in are just...*ugh.*"

"I'll put you in touch with my friend Philippe. He sources a lot of pieces from these underground artists."

"Is 'underground' code for failed?"

"Failed in life, sure, but not with their art," I say, feeling the tequila make me a more confident liar. "They need fast cash because they're destitute. They're brilliant, but threw their lives away for coke or booze or whores—sorry, sex workers."

"Oh my gosh, that's so *sad.*"

"Desperation fuels the best art," I murmur, as an LAPD helicopter soars overhead.

The cramping in my abs is bordering on unbearable, but I know my chance to seal the deal is close. I go in for the kill.

"I have a spare piece that could use a new home. Why don't you come downstairs to see if it's less 'ugh' than your prints?"

She checks her phone and clicks the side button to shut it off before sliding it into an Alo Yoga tote bag.

"You've got 30 minutes," Lana says, slipping into a gauzy white linen cover-up.

As we walk towards the elevator, I finally relax my abs and breathe normally, which makes me lightheaded for a second. The elevator arrives on the 14th floor and we walk down the hallway toward my room, carrying on a pointless conversation about how we found our maids. Even though Lana lives in the same building, she's awestruck when she steps into my living room, which has several new pieces: a Vladimir Kagan curved sofa, an Hervé van der Straeten coffee table, a pair of Ralph Pucci lounge chairs, a custom silk rug from Fedora Design. I paid my interior designer north of $50,000 for moments exactly like this: to erase any doubts that she can do better.

My custom walnut bookcase is lined with books, thick books, like *Infinite Jest* and *The Count of Monte Cristo* and Edward Gibbon's six-volume *History of the Decline and Fall of the Roman Empire*. I've read most of them cover to cover, some twice. If you asked me to recall the names of characters or explain why these books carry cultural significance, I probably wouldn't be able to do it. But I've read a lot of them, and that's more than most 27-year-olds can say.

"You've read *all* of these?" Lana asks, lugging my first edition copy of *Gravity's Rainbow* off the shelf.

"I actually met Thomas Pynchon at a party once…in the Hamptons," I lie.

"Who?" Lana asks, fanning the pages.

"Never mind. Does it surprise you that I read a lot?" I ask, probably a little too aggressively.

"No, no. I mean, you seem, I don't know, *smart?*"

"I think 'curious' is more accurate."

"Well, obviously you're a little book nerd. Do you think you would ever, like, write your own book one day?"

I let the question hang, tracing the book spines with my index finger.

"It's funny you ask," I say, pausing just long enough to make it seem like I'm weighing whether or not to let her in on a secret. "I actually started working on a novel on my flight back from Tulum." My chest tightens as I say it, but I keep my face blank and my voice even.

"Okay, that's kinda hot," she gushes. "So you're an author…what's your book about?"

As she slides all 776 pages of *Gravity's Rainbow* back onto the shelf, I realize this is the first time anyone has called me an author. My ego greedily devours the sweet sound of that title. I want her to say it again, say it a thousand times. Maybe someday I'll want to write more than I want casual sex with a girl who thinks authors are hot. But for now, I have to divert.

"Not sure I can trust you with that information," I say coolly. "Word around town is you're quite the socialite."

"So *funny*," she says sarcastically, rolling her eyes. "Fine, keep your masterpiece a secret."

A ray of sunlight hits Lana's skin through the window as she walks toward the featured art piece in my living room: a mixed media collage on canvas with enamel, oil, and acrylic paint by Alberto Ruiz, circa 2003, six months before he blew his brains out with a shotgun in an Albuquerque motel because his fiancée left him for a hedge fund manager. If my friend Philippe were real, he'd say the piece adds some much-needed warmth to the room.

While Lana stares at the art, I wrap my arms around her waist and nestle my chin between her shoulder and neck. I tell her the story about Alberto Ruiz shooting himself in the head in the Albuquerque motel, how they found his pinkish-gray brain splattered on the bathroom mirror. She says it's a shame how some of the most talented artists are also the most tormented.

I softly prod her shoulder with my chin and take her earlobe, diamond stud and all, between my teeth. I smell coconut lotion and minty-fresh breath and a hint of chlorine. I want all of it, all of her, and she wants all of me, too. We start towards the bedroom, tongues interlocked, as I rip off her bikini top. She licks, I bite, she sucks, I thrust, she moans. There are no traces of romance or affection. Not even close. We're animals using each other's bodies. I tell this to myself as I'm on top of her and beneath her and behind her, trying to fill a void that no mixed media collage or bottle of Krug champagne or apartment amenities can fill.

We climax, almost simultaneously, and I'm looking directly into Lana's eyes for the very first time. They're ice blue like the pool at the Four Seasons, except for a small, crescent-shaped black speck on her left iris.

"You look like an action figure," Lana says, giggling as she traces the ridges and valleys of my abdominal muscles.

"Powered by dirty martinis and Macallan 18," I say, flexing a little.

She bites my bottom lip, giggling, and rolls out of my bed. I look for tan lines but don't see any—her skin is a uniform coat of bronze. I watch her collect her sunglasses and phone, which she stares at blankly for a few seconds before slipping into her bikini and then the white cover-up.

"Let's skip the small talk next time," she tells me while tying up her hair.

"I wouldn't dare steal any more of your tanning time," I say, trying to find my swimsuit in the tangled sheets.

I watch her walk out of my room and hear her Prada flip-flops clacking across the white oak floors in my living room. I hear her open the door, exit the room, close the door. This is Lana's year of self-care. I'm lying in bed, suddenly shivering, and I don't want to feel alone, so I immediately open TikTok and start watching videos of a body modification addict with two tongues.

It's Wednesday at 3:27 in the afternoon and I have to meet my girlfriend, Sophia, at n/naka in a few hours—time to get my shit together.

Dinner with Sophia at n/naka

THE UBER DRIVER picks me up outside my apartment lobby in a shiny black Lincoln Navigator. I climb into the back row and the interior is, thankfully, spotless. God forbid I have to give another one-star review because of a dirty floor mat. My driver is a morbidly obese bald man who I'm guessing is either Serbian or Russian based on his accent. He breathes heavily, like a bulldog, and smells like acidic checkout-aisle cologne, which fails to mask the stench of cigarettes and a vague body odor.

"Hello, Nathan?"

"Yeah," I say, making sure I didn't scuff my Scarosso loafers.

"Heading to n/naka, correct?"

"Uh huh."

"Nice, it is a nice place, I've heard."

"Totally," I murmur.

n/naka—which I've been to twice—has two Michelin stars and is consistently ranked as one of the 50 best restaurants on planet Earth. The chef-owner is known for blending classical Japanese cooking techniques with the seasonality of California cuisine. The competition for reservations is so intense that most people give up and settle for something less impressive, like Morihiro or Kogane. n/naka releases reservations one month in advance on Sunday mornings at ten o'clock and if you don't refresh your web browser at the precise moment they go live, you're fucked. If you manage to get a table but don't confirm when they reach out two days beforehand, they cancel your reservation. My cousin Romona was late to her friend's baby shower because she was refreshing her computer at home—didn't trust the Wi-Fi anywhere else, and still didn't get in. Luckily, my dad's business partner knows a guy who can snag reservations on non-peak days, as long as I give him a 48-hour notice.

To kill time in the car, I'm re-reading reviews in *Condé Nast* and *The Los Angeles Times*. This helps me remember the appropriate language to use with the staff and what to expect during the meal so I don't accidentally embarrass myself. The critics use words like "conceptual" and "poetic" and "otherworldly." It will be an "elegant symphony" and I feel prepared. Out of curiosity, I check n/naka's most recent geotags on Instagram to see who's been there recently: a Turkish fashion model celebrating her 21st birthday, cast members from Bravo's hit new series *The Valley*, a food blogger from Seattle with 821 followers—an ensemble of desperate losers.

The Uber app says I'm still 23 minutes away, so I start picking at the skin around my thumbs—a habit I've had since kindergarten. The medical term is "dermatillomania," which psychologists classify as a form of obsessive-compulsive disorder and also a body-focused repetitive behavior. I do it to distract myself from anxiety, stress, and depression, but mainly to escape the unbearable boredom. Peeling off the small bits of flesh provides temporary relief, but the wounds make me self-conscious, creating a vicious cycle. I've done enough damage that the skin on both my thumbs is discolored to a pale pink hue, which contrasts with my tan hands. Sometimes I get so aggressive that blood pools around my nail bed, so I have to

wear Band-Aids when I leave the house. I've kept it under
control today so far, but I have two Band-Aids in my pocket in
case Sophia is in one of her moods.

We cross The Ten where traffic is at a standstill—an
endless stream of hot metal, bumper to fucking bumper.
Horns blare hopelessly, and if I look close enough, I can see
the drivers. Some stare at their phones, some dump pre-
packaged snacks into their mouths, some helplessly crane
their neck in search of a less congested route. But most of them
just stare blankly through their windshields, watching their
lives play out like a movie they've lost interest in.

We continue creeping down Overland, an
unremarkable street that runs through Palms. It's lined with
gas stations and strip malls, which are full of shops that are
somehow still in business: a cell phone and laptop repair store,
a lamp store, a notary service. The sidewalks are empty.
Walking on sidewalks in LA is humiliating.

My phone buzzes, snapping me out of my lull. Sophia:
"Almost there! Love youuu :)"

I start typing "same," but delete it and just like her
message because I'm more excited to explore the art of kaiseki
than I am to see my girlfriend. Which is absurd, since most
guys would torch their 401(k) just to sniff Sophia's underwear.
She's classically beautiful—think Audrey Hepburn. Curvy but
not lumpy. Toned but not bulky. Charming enough to hold a
conversation, but not smart enough to really challenge you. A
sense of style that's tasteful but seductive. A syrupy-sweet
personality that makes you feel like you've known her since
high school. Has an Instagram account for her Pomeranian.

She's just over a year into her job at Manuel-Ballard, a
fledgling interior design firm in West Hollywood, where she

hopes to eventually help celebrities and socialites bring their dream homes to life. Sophia and I have been dating for about eight months, although we disagree on when we officially became an item. She comes from a wealthy family (though not as wealthy as mine) in Santa Barbara and we're both young and our families think we can build a bright, beautiful future together and they're probably not wrong. But things are getting stale.

I tell the driver to stop at a green light to let me out by the restaurant, which is located between an addiction treatment center and a psychic offering $20 palm readings. I slide out of the Navigator, realizing I should have brought a flask of Macallan 18 to dull my emotions in the car. Sophia is waiting for me in front of the rock-and-bonsai garden at the entrance, using her phone's front camera as a mirror as she applies a fresh coat of ruby lipstick. She came straight from the office and she's wearing the houndstooth wool blazer I bought her from Nordstrom over a white Wesler top from The Row. Her shiny brown hair is pulled back into a tight ponytail and her perpetually tan face is bright and dewy. Sophia had mild-to-moderate acne in high school, so she's self-conscious about her complexion even though I've reassured her countless times that "it looks amazing, babe—better than the models."

She gives me a tired smile and we share a kiss. It tastes like vanilla.

"I swear, this dinner is the only thing that kept me going today," she says, exasperated.

"Another rough one?" I ask, somewhat disinterested.

"I can't even *talk* about it until I've had a drink."

We enter via the tobi-ishi-style walking path, which is paved with rocks collected from the California desert. The walking path is the most notable addition from the restaurant's recent interior makeover, led by a lauded Tokyo-based design firm. Inside, a timid Japanese man ushers Sophia and me into the main dining room: a severe, daring space encased by dark gray shikkui lime plaster. The center wall is covered in a handmade washi paper. A Japanese copper vase hangs in an arched opening. The space is filled with a reverent silence, as if we just walked into some sort of religious ceremony. We're seated in the corner of the dining room, a decent location given this was a relatively impromptu reservation. I settle into the black walnut chair before taking inventory of the other guests—an inconspicuous middle-aged couple, an overdressed Indian family, a party of four men, all of whom are wearing Rolex Yacht-Masters, and I get this feeling that one of them recognizes me.

The meal will be a three-hour, 13-course Kaiseki tasting menu with wines and artisanal sake pairings. For the two of us, it will run me $905 before tax and tip. n/naka is famous for never repeating dishes for returning guests. They keep huge binders filled with notes on every person that's dined here: what they ate, what they drank, whether they're left or right-handed so the staff know where to place the utensils. Sophia glances at my fingers as I pick up my water to see how much damage I've done. She breaks the silence with an unbearably banal anecdote.

"All I had to eat today was a Greek yogurt at 10 a.m. I'm *starving*."

"That's crazy, babe," I say, momentarily distracted by

the flash of an iPhone in my peripheral vision (must be a first timer). "You should've gotten that smoothie from Erewhon that you like—the strawberry probiotic one."

"You know I don't like that anymore. It has *xylitol* in it. And besides, I need to eat more complete protein. You know, because it makes me feel full longer?"

I can't tell if this is a statement or a question. Sophia always falls for these holistic health and wellness grifts, which combine some new dieting technique with career development and relationship skills—all under the guise of teaching young women how to get in touch with their true selves, heal from generational trauma, etc. Every few weeks, she'll adopt a new prism through which to view her life, and I'm inevitably lectured about how it's "actually legit." Last summer, she joined a clinic that specializes in IV therapy. Twice a week, she'd pump nicotinamide adenine dinucleotide (NAD) into her bloodstream, a coenzyme that she was convinced would stimulate cell regeneration and reverse her biological age to 22. She stopped after another member at the clinic had a mild seizure. A few months before that, she adopted something called "The Philosophy of 'No,'" which prompted her to decline invitations to parties, most of my sexual advances, anything with refined sugar, and alcohol. She stopped because her astrologer warned that it was disrupting the balance of her Jupiter in Libra.

While mindlessly chit-chatting—some minor variation of a conversation we've had a thousand times—a gaunt waiter in a suit jacket mercifully serves our first course: Sake Zuke, a grilled scallop with salmon eggs, and English pea soup. I eat, smile, nod, and agree with everything Sophia says throughout our meal. Every banal anecdote, every hollow cliche, every imaginary slight she thinks she's enduring. Sentences are exchanged, but I have no idea what I'm saying. I watch my own responses leave my mouth, untethered, meaningless. My body goes through the motions: lift my chopsticks to my mouth, raise my eyebrows to feign surprise, grimace at the right moments. I consider telling her the same story I told Lana about my nonexistent novel, just to see if I can make myself believe it's happening. But for now, Sophia is the soundtrack to my tasting menu.

Tsukuri sashimi. Her boss is cheating on his boyfriend with the new pool boy. Again.

A5 Miyazaki Wagyu. She's desperate to get her hair cut by Chris McMillan.

Shiizakana abalone spaghetti with summer truffles and cod roe. She saw Kaia Gerber and Austin Butler wearing matching Birkenstocks at the Malibu Country Mart.

Mushimono with crab, egg, and cherry blossom mochi rice. She may need to stop training for her half marathon because her patellar tendinitis is flaring up.

Zensai duck, fig, and ceviche. Her brother-in-law, Brent, is installing radiant floor heating in the new house he bought in Telluride. I remember meeting that douchebag at Mother Wolf with Sophia and her older sister Greer. Now I'm getting horrible flashbacks of his grimy little mustache, the stupid Japanese Kanji tattoo he plastered on his forearm because he stayed at an Airbnb in Tokyo for a week, and his obsession with name-dropping founders of worthless brands. These memories stew in my brain, nearly making me physically ill, until it finally dawns on Sophia during the tenth course that she hasn't asked me a single question tonight.

"Okay, yap sesh over," she declares with a single clap of the hands. "How was your Wednesday? You look *tan*."

"I was reading at the pool...after work," I say as my mind drifts to a panoramic shot of Lana slathering her heart-shaped ass with tanning oil.

"My little bookworm," she says, scrunching her nose.

I think back to how good it felt when Lana bestowed the title of 'author' to me, and I'm lusting for it again, so I put the bait out there.

"Someone asked me today—while I was at work—if I'd ever write my own book," I say, darting my eyes to see if the guys with the Yacht-Masters are eavesdropping. "I think I should do it."

Sophia's face goes blank before she flashes a delayed smile—the kind of smile you give a toddler who says he wants to be an astronaut or the point guard on the Lakers. She's probably more enthused about telling people she's dating an author than discussing character arcs or inciting incidents.

"S*lay*, babe, I can totally see you in your author era. We could throw the cutest book launch party, get you some stunning headshots—maybe you could even get your book made into a movie. You know, because of your dad and all?"

"They'll be rolling out the red carpet before we know it," I say drily, dragging my finger along the rim of my glass.

It's dark and probably cold outside, but I'm on the border of buzzed and drunk so I don't notice the temperature change. My abs are sore—I'm not sure whether it's from the Tabata workout I did this morning or from flexing them at the pool or from fucking Lana or all of the above. After Sophia finishes posting pictures of our meal to her Instagram story, she asks if I want to go back to her apartment in West Hollywood and watch *Selling Sunset* or maybe some reruns of *Friends*. I decline because I have an early workout tomorrow, so I pull out my phone and call an Uber.

"That's okay, babe, I understand," she says, making a fake pouty face. "Maybe next time?"

"Yeah, I promise, next time," I say, almost making the mistake of ordering an UberX instead of an Uber Black.

We share the same tight-lipped kiss we did three hours ago before she climbs into her white Audi Q7. She waves goodbye as she pulls onto Woodbine and I'm immensely grateful for the solitude.

My driver picks me up shortly after in a black Escalade, playing "Tempted" by Squeeze. I spend the fifteen-minute ride back to my apartment refreshing my email inbox, searching for something nonexistent. I tell the driver to roll down the window, but the wind messes up my hair and and even though nobody will see me I roll it back up and just stare at the back of the headrest, which goes in and out of focus.

I'm too exhausted to brush my teeth when I get home, so I collapse on my sofa and fall asleep watching a YouTube video where three friends bet $10,000 to see who can stay inside a porta potty the longest without throwing up.

Money

THE MONEY HITS my Citigold Private Client Checking Account on the last Tuesday of every month at 6 a.m. PST. The Citigold Package is an all-in-one banking setup for clients who park at least a million dollars, on average, across linked accounts: checking, savings, retirement, brokerage. I get the usual perks—elevated ATM withdrawal limits, fee waivers, a rotating cast of financial advisors and relationship managers, early access to investment products with names like "Global Equity Premium Select." There's also a guy named Rick who texts me if I accidentally overdraft.

My monthly deposit amount is $45,000, which is wired from a trust fund my parents set up for me the day I was born. The distribution terms stated that I would start getting monthly payments when I turned 22 years old, contingent on a bachelor's degree and a vague requirement of "gainful employment." Most other people I know with trust funds have to wait until their parents die before they see a cent. My dad thought it would be better to "teach me financial literacy" instead of "falling into money like a reprobate lottery winner." Something he said with a glass of Syrah and Fox News muted in the background.

My trust is revocable, meaning they can shut off the spigot if they choose to. I'm not really worried about that, considering I stay out of trouble and have generally kept their stress levels to a minimum for 27 years. Once they're gone, the trust becomes irrevocable and I'll inherit the total sum of the assets, which includes liquid cash, real estate holdings, stocks, bonds, mutual funds, ETFs, jewelry, artwork, vehicles, and partial ownership in a few LLCs with no websites. I'm not sure what the total value of the trust is, but based on some rough napkin math, my guess is that it's in the high eight figures.

As long as I don't commit a felony or start smoking crack, I'll never have to worry about money for the rest of my life. Neither will my kids or their kids. My parents have made half-hearted attempts to convince me that I don't actually need this money, that I would "do great" purely on my merit and natural gifts, and we both know that's not something we should put to the test.

I grew up in Palisades Hills, a manicured enclave engineered for safety, seclusion, and scenic beauty—quiet streets, elite schools, canyons that look good in stock photography and antidepressant commercials. The home I was raised in sat on a high ridge overlooking a winding road, where tourists sometimes parked to take pictures of sunsets. Prices range from two million for a barely livable two-bedroom ranch to $100 million for glass-and-concrete estates that people gawk at in tabloid magazines. Private security officers roam the streets because residents don't trust LAPD to protect their property from armed criminals. Our neighborhood was home to mostly retirees, business executives, entertainment professionals, and doctors seeking more space and fewer people—but nobody worth remembering.

My parents left Manhattan Beach in 1995, three months after I was born, and bought their new house on impulse. At the time, my dad had just become a founding partner at an entertainment law firm in Century City—the gig he still has today. He works long days (at least by Southern California standards) untangling contracts, fielding calls from desperate agents, and negotiating with studio heads with undiagnosed mood disorders. "Playing chess with billion-dollar egos," as he said. When my dad isn't at his office, he's on the golf course—hitting the driving range, meeting his instructor for private putting lessons, or playing 18 holes with some executive from HBO or Paramount. One of his proudest achievements was getting into the Riviera Country Club, which (I'm frequently reminded) ranks among the most exclusive clubs in America with members including Hugh Grant, Mark Wahlberg, and Tom Brady. His initiation fee was rumored to be north of $300,000, which he mentions constantly.

My dad grew up in Sherman Oaks, the son of a physicist who founded and sold nine biomedical companies over the course of three decades. Despite having more money than they could spend, the family lived modestly. One house, one car, one TV. But my dad's post-collegiate success at the firm turned him into a *bon vivant* with a restless passion to collect the best versions of whatever he could get his hands on. Luxury timepieces, an ever-expanding wine cellar, a rotating fleet of vintage Porsches, custom suits shipped to our house from Italian tailors. In his younger years, my dad was so immaculately groomed that his coworkers thought he was gay. He got a hair transplant in his early forties and religiously got manicures and facials before metrosexuality was normalized in the 2000s. He said the other lawyers at his firm were assholes—emotionally stunted frat boys who cheated on their wives with naive assistants and skipped their kids' tee ball games to play poker and treated valets like animals. But my dad was, and still is, what I believe to be a halfway decent guy. I think. He was too busy to be the mentor type of father. Our relationship was mostly devoid of corporal bonding experiences like teaching me how to ride a bike, string a tennis racket, tie a tie, throw a spiral, or mow the lawn. But he believed in the power of grand experiences, delayed gratification, and, when pressed, maybe even God.

My mom is a pediatric cardiologist who graduated from Stanford with honors. Her father and grandfather were both doctors in the Bay Area, so it was expected of her to carry on the family tradition since she was the firstborn. She racked up a stronger resume than both of them combined. On top of directing the Division of Pediatric Cardiology at Cedars-Sinai, she sits on the boards of a bunch of philanthropic organizations and routinely jets off to third-world countries to provide free medical services to disease-ridden children. Her only flaw is her compulsive need to surround herself with people. The idea of being alone always gave her a sense of dread, which she remedied by filling her calendar with social obligations. I remember her hosting elaborate dinner parties at our house, preparing dishes like duck à l'orange and bouillabaisse from scratch. The women who came to our house—mostly housewives or intentionally vague "fashion people"—would drone on about shows like *American Idol, Big Brother*, and *The Real Housewives of Beverly Hills* while my mom quoted Susan Sontag, Joan Didion, and Kate Chopin. She believed in longevity, the transformative power of the arts, and gratitude. Above all, she believed in paving a safe path for me. Her son. Her only child. Her legacy.

I was always mature for my age, or that's what I was told. Some relatives and close family friends said that I was born a grown man. I followed rules. I made my bed with military precision every morning, smoothing out the wrinkles on my duvet cover. My hair was always neatly parted to the left. I never talked back, never questioned authority. I shared my organic dried mango with my classmates at the lunch table. I said "yes ma'am," "yes sir," "please," and "thank you." I ate my vegetables and washed my plates before putting them in the dishwasher and read stacks of books, even ones that weren't assigned to me. I asked smart questions, withheld stupid ones, and used words I picked up from my dad's phone calls that sounded sophisticated. I was a "good boy" with parents whom I was "lucky to have." And aside from my habit of tearing away the skin around my fingernails until they stained my bedsheets with blood, I had an idyllic childhood.

My parents were obsessed with being well-traveled and getting out of our bubble in the Palisades. They planned multiple family vacations every year. By the time I was fourteen, I had visited Paris, London, Rome, Tokyo, Barcelona, Stockholm, Sydney, and several Caribbean islands. We took ski trips to Vail and fishing trips to Clearwater. I visited art galleries and watched plays and went to symphonies. I listened to Chopin and Duke Ellington and Bill Evans on our record player. I ate escargot and jamón Ibérico and foie gras and other things I couldn't understand or pronounce, but knew I was supposed to appreciate because of the numbers on the menus.

I attended a private, Catholic day school and had personal tutors for most of my subjects, even though my teachers assured my parents I was "doing great." I made mostly straight As and scored in the 97th percentile on my standardized tests. My motive wasn't to become smarter or enrich myself, but simply just to do well, to bring home numbers on pieces of paper that convinced my parents I was worth something. I attended a private, Catholic, all-boys prep school where I made the honor roll, played varsity tennis all four years (despite chronic rotator cuff tendinitis), and was elected to the student council. I took up chess during my sophomore year and got just good enough to understand what it might look like to be elite, but I quit after nine months because I couldn't be as good as I felt like I needed to be to be admired. I wasn't particularly funny or charismatic, but I looked the part and had the right opinions and behaved the right way, so I had no problem assimilating with the upper echelon.

After a year of intense tutoring with a Korean woman named Georgianne, I scored 1450 on the S.A.T., applied to UCLA early decision, and got accepted. My parents encouraged me to attend a school outside of California, or at least outside of Los Angeles. I had plenty of options given my grades, test scores, extracurricular activities, and strings my parents were willing to pull. I explained that I wanted to go to UCLA because my goal was to be an entertainment lawyer like my dad, and that UCLA would give me the best opportunity to forge relationships and land internships at law firms around Los Angeles. I reminded them that millions of eighteen-year-olds across the world would kill to attend UCLA and I shouldn't throw away the opportunity just because the campus was six miles away from our house.

I spent my four years at UCLA pretending that I shared the same interests as my peers. Beer pong, tailgates, getting my dick sucked by girls I had no interest in. I auditioned for the role of "normal dude" and I succeeded. I reluctantly settled on

English as my major because that's what my dad chose, doing the bare minimum to maintain my scholarship, and it quickly became clear that law school wasn't in the cards—at least not one my parents would be proud of. At the time, I was watching *Mad Men* and convinced myself I could become the West Coast version of Draper—getting paid to day drink in a glass office and convince people to buy poison they don't need with money they don't have. Once my dad realized I wouldn't be the heir to his entertainment law empire, he called in a favor from one of his golf buddies who was on the Board of Advisors at an advertising agency called KBM. Two weeks later, I was at a welcome party for incoming interns, wondering if I'd ever be able to make as much money as my dad.

The narrative I was sold—and blindly regurgitated for so long—was that money expanded your options, turned the world into a video game that you played on easy mode until you got the life you wanted. But as I've crept into my late twenties, my monthly deposits have had the opposite effect, hemming me into a safe, predictable position that nobody gives a shit about. I can't recall a single instance over the past 27 years where I felt like I had earned anything that might resemble respect, aside from a few dinner party conversations where I appeared to impress strangers by explaining something like the difference between caramelization and the Maillard reaction. But even then, I imagined those people murmuring behind my back, *of course he knows that—he's a spoiled prick*.

You sound deranged when you try to explain this to people who are crippled with debt, clipping coupons to save a dollar on paper towels or paying for their DoorDash meals in installments, but it's true: Easy money anesthetizes you. It lulls you to sleep like a Klonopin washed down with vodka, and by the time you wake up the gap between who you are and who you want to be is too wide to bridge.

Shrink

"HAVE YOU BEEN taking the medication?" Dr. Alper asks, scrawling something on a yellow legal pad.

"Sometimes," I murmur, shutting my eyes. "Most of the time."

"It's very important that you take it daily," he says with barely a pause, almost carelessly. "It can take several weeks for the effects to kick in."

Dr. Alper is the psychiatrist I just started seeing on Wednesday evenings. My parents basically mandated that I get a shrink after I made an offhand comment at my cousin's graduation party that I "might pull a Kurt Cobain" if my flight to Milan got delayed like it did last year. Dr. Alper came highly recommended by my family's primary care physician. My 50-minute sessions cost $600.

The medication Dr. Alper is referring to is Effexor (venlafaxine), a serotonin-norepinephrine reuptake inhibitor, which is supposed to improve my mood, ease my anxiety, and restore my interest in daily living. The peach-colored capsules, when I take them, give me a fleeting sense of calm and control, which might be psychosomatic. But they also give me vicious headaches, nausea, and diarrhea. Most recently, I've noticed that the pills nuke my libido and make it harder to come, so I end up skipping my dose more often than not. I'm not supposed to drink while taking Effexor, but I do it anyway because alcohol makes me feel better than the drug.

Dr. Alper's office is located on the 13th floor inside a gated tower in Century City. It's small but tasteful and looks more like a home study than a shrink's office: mid-century aesthetic, lots of earth tones and clean lines. There's a tall, angular cactus by the window, which I'm just now noticing has its thorns removed. I catch a whiff of sage. I'm slouched in a giant but overly stiff mahogany swivel chair, eyeing a statue of a miniature blue horse on the shelf behind Dr. Alper's shiny bald head, which has an irregularly shaped birthmark on the crown. I'm sure the horse is supposed to represent something, maybe the wild spirit of the American west, but I can't summon the energy to ask. My eye twitches. A drop of blood slides down my thumb. I wipe it on the chair.

After a painfully long staring match, he says, "I don't think your parents would be happy to know you're ignoring medical advice since they're paying for your sessions."

High-Intensity Interval Training

A SPASM OF ANXIETY wakes me up at 5:57 a.m. I'm always up between two and five minutes before my 6 a.m. alarm, and with that spare time I stare at the back of my eyelids and pretend today is the day something changes. I'm reeling from a headache, thanks to the Weller 12 Year I drank myself to sleep with last night (I forgot to drink my alkaline water before bed). I have an irresistible urge to check my phone, which is on Do Not Disturb, resting next to my head. I've tried to break this habit over the past few years, but I'm powerless. This machine, this pocket-sized supercomputer, dictates my every waking hour. My hands are shaking like a fentanyl addict coming down from a high and I'm fucking powerless. The phone wins again today. I unlock the screen with Face ID, and my eyes are flooded with blue light that amplifies my headache to a degree that I'm barely willing to tolerate.

Emails.

My Tom Ford Tuscan Leather cologne is arriving today.

Sandro is having a flash sale on their outerwear collection for VIP customers.

UCLA wants money for a scholarship fund.

News.

A novel narrated by a nonbinary, antifascist subway rat in New York is an early contender for Best Book of the Year.

The U.S. Navy featured a drag queen in its latest recruitment video.

Subaru is helping deaf children enjoy Yosemite National Park.

Reminders.

Personal training appointment at 7:30.

Make a reservation at Providence for Sophia's birthday.

Start writing chapter one of the novel.

I unravel myself from a cocoon of linen sheets and head to the bathroom, dragging my feet on the cool hardwood floors. I turn on the light and study myself in the mirror from all angles. My skin, evenly tanned from an especially sunny fall, is supple and almost completely hairless, except for the tufts coming from my armpits. I refocus on my face: pale blue hunter eyes, pouty lips, lush brows, angular cheekbones, a chiseled jawline. I force myself to smile and see dimples. My deltoids, pectorals, and obliques are chiseled, but in a natural, tasteful way—I want to impress people, not scare them.

My biggest concern is my hair. Despite being thick and adequately moisturized, I've noticed the corners of my hairline beginning to recede slightly into the shape of an M. It's unnoticeable to everyone except for me. Sophia assured me it's all in my imagination, but I notice she'll take quick glances at the areas I'm self-conscious about. A few weeks ago, I paid for a $750 consultation with a Persian dermatologist in Beverly Hills who specializes in follicular unit extraction (FUE) hair transplant procedures. He told me to come back in six months. I asked for a finasteride prescription, but he said the potential side effects (decreased libido, delayed ejaculation, depression) would outweigh the potential benefits at my stage. So now I inspect my hair for a good two minutes every morning, running my fingers through it and parting different areas to locate areas of concern. I look at my pillowcase for shedding.

I study my brush to see if it's accumulated more loose hairs than normal. As I perform these rituals, I tell myself that I would be a confident, happy man without hair—a blatant lie. I look at my fingers one by one. The cuticles have partially healed over with pink, delicate skin that likely won't last past noon today.

After a long piss, I walk into the kitchen and drink 18 ounces of filtered water before starting my daily supplement regimen: 20 grams of collagen peptides to support skin elasticity, 1,000 mg of Omega-3 fish oil for joint health, four hair growth nutraceutical capsules, three grams of nootropic powder for cognitive and memory support, three probiotic capsules for digestive support, two full-spectrum, delayed-release multivitamin capsules to fill any nutritional gaps, and an additional 1500 IU of vitamin D3. Lastly, I brush my teeth with a fluoride-free toothpaste that's infused with hydroxyapatite and 1.2 micrograms of sublingual vitamin B12 for natural energy support.

I put on my workout clothes (tank top and shorts from Alo, Cloudrift shoes from On) before heading out to my wellness club, tempus. There's really no point for me to belong to a wellness club since my apartment has a two-story gym, two pools (a 75-foot indoor lap pool and an outdoor lounge pool lined with cabanas), a tennis court, and a full-service spa. There are also indoor and outdoor theaters, a game room with a wet bar, a one-acre private park, 24/7 private security, and a robot butler that delivers meals and packages to my doorstep. Pretty much everything from dry cleaning to private pickleball lessons to Reiki healings to Botox appointments can be booked and managed via the property's mobile app. Sometimes I'll run into men dressed in tight-fitting blazers wandering through the building and shouting things like "big billski" or "we're not running a charity here." Or I'll see surgically-enhanced women in yoga clothes pushing their French bulldogs in Bugaboo strollers around the private park, quietly complaining to someone on the phone about minorities committing crimes.

The morning air is chilly, but I don't mind because tempus is just a short jog down Santa Monica. I put in my AirPods and play Today's Hits—the first song is about a guy who has hoes in multiple area codes. It's an abomination, but preferable to listening to my own thoughts. I start slowly, waiting for the stiffness in my legs to subside. The street is quiet except for a few early risers heading to their own rituals, faces drawn with a mix of anticipation and dread. A homeless man, enveloped in a dirt-caked blanket, is sprawled on a bench with an advertisement for Kylie Cosmetics.

As I slow to a walk near the gym entrance, catching my breath, the music swells to a crescendo, perfectly timed with my arrival. I stroll into the reception area, an opulent space with European inflections like herringbone floors, salmon-hued floral wallpaper, caramel-leather couches, a wooden credenza, a stone fireplace, Frank Gehry Wiggle chairs, and lots of healthy plants. It was designed by some agency from Berlin and the aesthetic, according to a profile in *Vogue*, is called eclectic minimalism. Nadia, the concierge who's an aspiring comedian, greets me but I can't hear her because my AirPods are still in Noise Cancellation mode so I just nod and force my mouth into a tight-lipped grin. Three outrageously fit women in their early twenties (one with so much lip filler that her upper lip nearly touches her nose) with foundation-caked faces and neon-pink sports bras exit without a drop of sweat between them. "Everybody Loves the Sunshine" by Roy Ayers plays on the Bose speakers.

My monthly membership at tempus costs $750 per month. The five-story, 64,000 square-foot space has dedicated spaces for cardio, free weights, stretching, functional, and machine strength training in addition to classes like heated mat Pilates, barre sculpt, boxing, rhythm ride, compound strength, tabata interval training, metabolic boost, and the ever-popular Power Hour. All of the equipment can be seamlessly integrated with the tempus app. Aside from fitness amenities, tempus has a spa that offers targeted massages, mechanical lymphatic drainage, IV therapy, and three tiers of HydraFacials. There's a restaurant on the top floor that focuses on dishes with anti-inflammatory and cognitive benefits, including wild Pacific salmon, chan chan yaki, shiitake mushroom larb, roasted squash agnolotti, and nutritional yeast popcorn. There's also a meditation room, but people mostly use it to take naps or scroll through TikTok.

I walk upstairs to meet with Oliver, my personal trainer, on the Strength Floor. Oliver is muscular, but not as lean as I am. He has veneers and a smooth, almost feminine face with no traces of facial hair. He moved to LA from a decrepit suburb of Kansas City five years ago to pursue a career in acting and/or modeling. So far, he's been in a few ads for a new brand of functional almond butter and had a few lines in an independent romcom last year, which he was not paid for. He lives with three roommates in a dingbat somewhere off West Pico. I don't really need Oliver to train me, but every time I think about ditching him, I get anxious that I'll devolve into a fat, disgusting, undesirable slob.

"What's up, boss man?" he asks. "You ready to get after it?"

"Yeah," I murmur, distracted by an ethnically ambiguous girl doing hip thrusts in an outfit that could pass as a bathing suit.

I don't actually enjoy exercising, but since I have a pathological need to be seen as a physical specimen, I have no choice but to make it a daily priority. Unlike most people who are motivated by the health benefits and mental clarity that exercise provides, I'm motivated by a paralyzing fear of exceeding 10% body fat. And so I go to a different place in my head, willing my body to squat, push, pull, jump, and slam with the required maximal effort. Oliver needlessly barks words like "push," "move," "faster," "good," and "harder." I catch a glimpse of my rippling deltoid in the mirror, perfectly positioned under soft overhead lighting, and I almost break a smile.

After finishing off my workout, I do a quick stretch, trying to make eye contact with the ethnically ambiguous girl, but some desperate loser wearing zebra print parachute pants and a Malibu Sleaze trucker hat blocks my line of sight. Once I realize it's her boyfriend, I walk upstairs to the dry sauna. It's 165 degrees and smells like cedarwood and sweat. Some generic spa-core string music leaks through heat-proof Bose speakers. I try to relax, but my breath is jagged, my pulse erratic. Sweat beads on my chest, then my neck, torso, arms, and legs—like I'm being slowly dissolved.

I try to count my breaths but lose track after two. I try to track the movement of my diaphragm, but get distracted looking at my abs. I close my eyes, but some subconscious force peels them back open. I try to watch my thoughts, like

Dr. Alper told me, as if they were clouds passing through the sky. I decide this charade is fucking pointless, and as the sweat spots on the cedarwood fade, so does my fleeting desire to work on myself.

Work

"NO, NO, NO, absolutely not," says Brooke, desperately trying to preserve her veneer of professionalism. "Their CMO would never give us the green light on something so raunchy. You know better."

Brooke is a Senior Account Manager and she's been going at it with Aaron, the Associate Creative Director, for the last 15 minutes. Brooke is a rule-follower and a people pleaser who got straight As and had perfect attendance all through college and pays her taxes on time every year without looking for loopholes. Her neuroticism and relentless need for control are infuriating. But if they didn't have people like Brooke here, everything would come crashing down within 24 hours. Aaron, on the other hand, is allergic to authority and has a microscopic attention span and nearly flunked out of UC Irvine—twice. I wouldn't go as far as saying he's smart, but he has a decent grip on reality and that's more than anyone else here brings to the table.

We work together at KBM (Klingler, Brown, and Mattheson), where I've been the Executive Creative Director for a little over a year and a half. KBM is an "independent, global creative company that transforms some of the world's most well-known brands through bold, culture-changing, value-driving ideas."

Translated: advertising agency.

The original office is in Manhattan, but there are satellite branches in Los Angeles, Miami, Chicago, London,

Tokyo, Sydney, and Mexico City. I started at KBM as an Intern when I was a senior at UCLA. The interview was mostly a formality, since one of my dad's golf buddies was on the agency's Board of Advisors at the time. My first boss, Reza, was a Senior Copywriter with a barely-under-control Vicodin problem. He gushed over every line of copy I wrote or tagline I pitched—no matter how half-baked or banal—to sling mass-produced junk like diet cola, Bluetooth headphones, and antacid tablets. Everybody knew Reza was gay and wanted to fuck me, hence my cakewalk that summer. Regardless, KBM offered me a full-time job as a Junior Copywriter as soon as I graduated. Over the next few years, I was promoted to Copywriter, then Senior Copywriter, then Associate Creative Director, then Senior Creative Director, and finally to my current role as Executive Creative Director. A bunch of KBM lifers thought my acceleration through the ranks was a textbook case of nepotism. But they failed to realize that most of these promotions happened *after* my dad's golf buddy was voted off the Board of Advisors after he allegedly "honked" the breasts of a Senior Partner's wife at the agency's holiday party—an allegation he vehemently denied on the grounds that "it would make no sense for me to sexually harass anyone because I have erectile dysfunction."

KBM is on retainer with a bunch of global brands, including sneaker companies, automotive manufacturers, and fast food chains. They've won thousands of industry awards, and it's estimated they've generated trillions of dollars in collective value for these corporations and their shareholders, although nobody seems to know how that's quantified. As the Executive Creative Director, my job is basically to make up ideas that convince people to buy products. My base salary is $245,000 per year (not including bonuses).

As of this past week, I'm supposed to come up with a campaign for the second-best-selling Toothpaste Conglomerate in America. They made $15.96 billion in gross revenue last year, a four percent increase year-over-year. Now the board members and shareholders refuse to settle for number two any longer, so they're giving KBM (along with three rival agencies) a chance to help them take a "big swing" that will dethrone the incumbent king of the toothpaste aisle and help them become Number One.

As I'm deciding whether to finish what's left of my lukewarm coffee from Verve, Brooke hands me a stack of documents labeled "Market Research." I shudder at the energy it would take to read, much less comprehend, the multitude of graphs, charts, and blocks of 10-point text. The gist, from what I've pieced together, is that the Toothpaste Conglomerate is desperate to connect with young consumers—people my age—and their CMO is willing to take a "big swing" to make it happen. This target audience needs a toothpaste that makes them feel understood in a sea of nameless, faceless corporations. They need a toothpaste that gives them a sense of belonging. They need a toothpaste that's good for their body and better for the environment. They need a toothpaste that stands for important and progressive sociopolitical causes, including women's reproductive rights, racial justice, affordable housing, and gender-affirming healthcare. They need a toothpaste that will help them achieve enlightenment. They need to find happiness and fulfillment inside a tube of toothpaste. This is what the Market Research document says and it's a problem, a huge fucking problem, because the target audience doesn't view the Toothpaste Conglomerate in this light. In fact, it's the opposite. This is the toothpaste their parents, grandparents, and great-grandparents have used for more than a century to scrub the instant coffee stains off their teeth. They think this toothpaste is unprincipled and regressive and potentially carcinogenic. They don't believe this toothpaste stands for anything besides maximizing value for its shareholders.

Aaron is spinning in his chair, air-drumming with two Expo markers. "It's gotta be something about sex," he says, as if this were obvious. "You can't get laid if your breath smells like straight-up ass."

Brooke squeezes her eyes shut and tilts her head back. She's about to lose her mind.

"Aaron, we've been over this a million times."

"I'm not saying we have to shoot a hardcore gangbang to sell a tube of toothpaste," he says, kicking a pair of scuffed Adidas Sambas onto the conference table. "I'm saying we need something more provocative than a pasty white Karen-ass housewife and her loser daughter standing in front of a mirror brushing their teeth together like a couple psychopaths."

"They want to be a family-friendly brand," Brooke says, failing to mask her exasperation.

Aaron doodles a pair of comically huge tits on the whiteboard.

"The people we have to sell this shit to are more interested in getting their rocks off than preserving the nuclear family."

I'm pulling a hangnail on the outside of my right thumb and can't tell if it's going to bleed or come off clean. I check the clock—11:34. This was supposed to end at 11:30. I decide that if the meeting lasts more than two more minutes, I'll fake a migraine and leave.

"What did that one broad say?" Aaron asks. "She wants a big hit?"

"That *broad* is their CMO and she wants to take a *big swing*," says Brooke.

"That's rich coming from someone who shelled out five million bucks for a Super Bowl ad that said — what did it say? — 'do more for your mouth.' Fucking geniuses."

Brooke closes her MacBook and rubs her temples. She flashes me this helpless look and asks what I think we should do. I tell her we should go to lunch because there's always a line at the Japanese spot I want to go to once the noon rush hits.

Brooke, Aaron, and I walk to a discreet sushi restaurant on Wilshire. We pass a psychic, a costume jewelry shop, a marijuana dispensary, an assisted living facility for Iranian Jews. The sun is being suffocated by smog, and the sidewalk is empty except for a gruesomely sunburned homeless man screaming at a food delivery robot. None of us can understand what he's saying, but he looks to be either schizophrenic or under the influence of some sort of amphetamine or both, so we cross over to the other side of the street.

A cranky hostess wearing an N95 face mask seats us by the window, where I can see the homeless man around the corner, who is now wandering into oncoming traffic with what looks like a brick or a large rock. I'm starving and I know exactly what I want, so I ask if we can order right away. The hostess nods her head and mutters something I don't understand. I can tell Brooke feels rushed because she's gripping the menu to the point that her nail beds are white and she's pursing her lips while her green eyes dart around the various sections of sushi, hand rolls, and sashimi.

If I didn't know Brooke and saw her walking down the street, I probably wouldn't give her a second look. Her figure is unremarkable: a small and slightly lopsided ass, B cups in the early stages of sagging, a low waist-to-hip ratio, shoulder-length amber hair with noticeable split ends, and milk-white skin despite living in near-perpetual sunshine (she's paranoid about skin cancer because her dad died of melanoma last year, so she applies SPF 100 sunscreen any time she steps outside). And yet, after spending years in close proximity to Brooke at KBM, I can't help but feel some sort of vague connection to her. It's not so much of a physical or emotional or intellectual attraction as it is an attraction to my familiarity with her. The predictable cadence of her footsteps, the low, almost raspy pitch of her voice, her small coughs and delicate chews, the way she types and sneezes, the faint smell of aloe from her Gold Bond hand cream.

Most people think they're attracted to novelty, someone who can open their heart and mind, liberate them from life's suffocating monotony. But we always crawl back to the safe, familiar noise. Psychologists have a term for this—it's called the Proximity Bias. I learned about it on a podcast when I was flying to London to watch Wimbledon last summer.

Brooke is from some lifeless suburb outside of Dallas and went to the University of Texas, where she dropped out of her sorority after a semester and proceeded to graduate summa cum laude. Unlike most people at KBM, Brooke actually majored in advertising with minors in creative writing and comparative literature. She was hired the same week I was and also started her career as a Junior Copywriter but quickly switched to a Junior Account Manager because the HR department offered her a $3,000 raise. She shares a 900-square-foot dump in Sawtelle with two roommates and she's frantically trying to find a "serious boyfriend" who can "match her level of maturity" and with whom she can "settle down." Whenever Brooke whines about the LA dating scene, I can't help but think she just needs to slug a few martinis and get laid. But instead I nod and tell her to just keep putting herself out there.

A disheveled waiter who looks like he just rolled out of bed ambles over our table. Before he has a chance to take out his notepad, I rattle off my order: edamame, yellowtail sashimi, albacore nigiri, and a salmon skin roll. I almost tack on a bottle of sake but restrain myself. Aaron orders next, followed by Brooke, then I attempt to follow a jumbled dialogue about a C-list actor who was shot in the face by a catalytic converter thief outside Rossoblu in the Fashion District last night while I think of quotes I can use for the epigraph of my novel.

"So, did you guys hear we're getting a new group of interns in January?" Brooke asks, clearly desperate to pivot from the topic of bullets to the face. She's mixing wasabi and soy sauce together with her chopsticks, tragically unaware that she's tainting the soy sauce *and* ruining the aroma of the wasabi.

My interest in talking about potential interns is so infinitesimally small that I can't formulate a response, so I just sit there, letting a piece of yellowtail dissolve in my mouth before Aaron finally breaks the silence.

"Do we really need brain-dead college kids taking up space and drinking our coffee?" he asks, sucking on an edamame shell.

"Maybe *need* isn't the right word," Brooke says, blushing slightly. "But it never hurts to have a few extra hands around the office. They can dig into market trends, proofread decks, make sure the printer has enough paper—you know, the stuff you complain about. We're helping them build their résumés, too."

"The two chicks that interned with us last summer spent all day shopping online and snorting coke in the bathroom."

"And now they're both getting their real estate licenses, so you don't have to worry about them taking your share of the coffee, Aaron."

"I wouldn't mind seeing the one again—what was her name? Sarah? The one with the cans?"

Brooke sighs.

"Samara."

I feel a drop of excitement that swells into something I might call hope. A fresh batch of hot female interns could transform KBM's office from a corporate hellscape into a sexual fantasyland that I might legitimately want to work overtime at. I experienced it last summer with Samara—the naive, youthful energy, the nebulous sexual tension, the inescapable power dynamic. She would hover around my office, pretending to need something, then blush when I held her gaze just a second too long. It was almost sweet, like watching a deer wander onto a freeway, unaware of the inevitability of its fate. The idea of all of this returning makes my dick jump underneath my napkin. I'm already picturing the rush I'll get from telling Sophia I was working late on a campaign for a new squeezable cheese product when I was really emptying my balls into a junior at Pepperdine bent over my desk, covering her mouth so the janitor doesn't look inside.

"Who's in the running this year?" I ask, trying to conceal my eagerness.

"Yeah, any babes?" Aaron adds.

"Alessio told me Krause's nephew is interviewing next week," she says, referring to Scott Krause, one of KBM's Vice Presidents.

"Fuck yeah, just what we need, another nepo baby," Aaron murmurs.

Nepo baby. My vague horniness morphs into irritability and I notice I'm clutching my chopsticks tighter that usual. I'm pretty sure Aaron wasn't making a passive aggressive dig at me. But then again, he did have to basically suck the hiring manager's cock just to get his foot in the door, so maybe he subconsciously hates me for having an inside connection (even though I didn't need it). I retreat inward, my mind on the defensive, reminding myself that I would have climbed the ranks at KBM based on merit alone. This takes a lot of effort so I've lost my appetite. There's an entire salmon roll on a plate in front of me but I leave it untouched and ask our waiter for the check, which he carelessly drops on our table and before he has a chance to walk away I hand him my American Express Business Platinum credit card without checking the bill.

On the walk back to our office, we see the homeless man again, this time passed out against a rusty dumpster in an alleyway with his jeans around his swollen ankles. Brooke is trying to make small talk, but her sentences keep drifting off because she can't stop staring.

I spend the rest of the afternoon walking aimlessly around the office with my AirPods in, pretending like I'm on a call, trying to hear if anyone's talking about Scott Krause's nephew. But instead everyone is babbling about the importance of getting the Toothpaste Conglomerate's business. They proudly use jargon like "market share" and "customer persona" and "brand voice" and "key performance indicator." Some of them use these words because they want to impress their coworkers and others use them because they genuinely believe they matter, which is worse. I tune all of it out and spend the next hour and a half trying to find Krause's nephew on Instagram, Facebook, Twitter, LinkedIn, and Snapchat, but eventually go down a rabbit hole stalking Samara's new boyfriend—some slip-and-fall lawyer in Glendale who apparently thinks Ferragamo belts are impressive.

At 3:10 I leave the office, as I have done most days since becoming the Executive Creative Director, without anyone saying a word. The other employees at KBM, especially the senior-level ones, used to make passive aggressive quips like "Heading out this soon?" or "Calling it quits already?" I would always just reply, sternly and matter-of-factly, "Yes" before stepping into the elevator and putting on my sunglasses. I learned early on that the more effort I spent trying to explain my behavior, the less serious people took me. But if I simply acted like I deserved respect—regardless of whether I had earned it—they had no option but to give it to me.

When I get back to my apartment, I stop by the mail room where I retrieve my Tom Ford Tuscan Leather cologne, a newsletter from Beverly Hills Porsche about next year's new vehicle lineup, and a Save the Date card for my cousin's wedding in Oʻahu, which I throw in the trash. As I enter my room I'm faced with menacing silence and boredom, which I combat by masturbating, mechanically and efficiently, before taking a scalding hot shower. After toweling off, I try to lie down for a quick nap, but quickly realize I'm not tired because of the coffee I drank earlier, so I reluctantly call Providence to make a reservation for Sophia's birthday.

It's 4:37 and I have nothing to do the rest of the night. I was supposed to go to a screening in West Hollywood for some indie horror film about a dentist who tortures her patients to death, which Sophia's friend directed, but I declined because "work is really taking a toll on me." I force myself to sit in front of my computer and, once closing out my Pornhub tab, make a pathetic attempt at becoming a novelist.

Shrink

"DO YOU ALWAYS clench your fists?" Dr. Alper asks, slowly crossing his legs.

"What?" I snap, trying to see what kind of loafers he's wearing.

"Your fists," Dr. Alper says again, gesturing to my hands with a pair of horn-rimmed Oliver Peoples glasses. "Do you usually clench them when you're sitting around?"

"I don't know…maybe?"

I look out the window to my right. I can't see very far because the smog is thick today, so I shift my gaze to Dr. Alper's bookcase. *Memories, Dreams, Reflections* by Carl Jung; *Intuitive Thinking as a Spiritual Path* by Rudolf Steiner; *Superiority and Social Interest* by Alfred Adler. There's a small, bronze statue of a sitting Buddha on the middle row, serving as a bookend for a leather-bound encyclopedia collection.

"Do you remember clenching your fists as a kid?" he asks before resting his chin on his fist.

"If I don't remember doing it two seconds ago, how the fuck would I remember doing it as a kid?"

Dr. Alper quietly writes something on his notepad, and for the next 42 minutes, he lectures me about stress management techniques. One of them is to take five deep breaths—in through my nose, out through my mouth—if I notice my mind start to wander away from the present moment. Genius.

Dominic Vaiana

On the way out, he hands me a cognitive restructuring worksheet to help me "challenge irrational or illogical thoughts." As I exit the lobby, I crumple the worksheet and throw it in the trash, shifting my focus to how much alcohol I'll need to make it through Sophia's birthday dinner tonight.

Birthday Dinner for Sophia at Providence

AFTER WINNING AN ARGUMENT about whether the megachurch that Sophia wants to start attending is a cult operated by tax-evading grifters (it is), our Uber finally pulls up to Providence. It's one of three Michelin-star restaurants in LA that I haven't tried—the other two being Sushi Inaba and Mélisse. The consensus among food critics is that Providence serves the most innovative seafood dishes in North America, if not the world. It's in Hollywood, on Melrose, between a party supply store and a self-service car wash. The head chef has his own garden on the second floor, where he harvests his own edible florals. I studied the reviews at work yesterday. *Forbes* described the food as "intoxicating," "intricately orchestrated," and "revelatory," although I have a hard time trusting *Forbes* because their food editors led me astray with their glowing review of Osteria Moretti, which was a complete waste of $427.

I'd normally be happy or at least complacent in a restaurant like Providence, but I'm stuck with Sophia's bestie, Celeste, who she met at a breathwork retreat in Malibu a few summers ago, and her new boyfriend Felix who she met at Venice Run Club. I'm already on edge because they didn't apologize for showing up 13 minutes late, nearly violating the grace period and ruining the whole night.

Felix is an associate producer for a cable TV network that makes unscripted reality shows about the sex lives of Siamese twins, autistic couples, virgins who masturbate to cars, and people so morbidly obese they have to get airlifted out of their homes so they can have gastric bypass surgery. His uncle, the Senior Vice President of Development at the network, handed him the job even though his only prior experience was making failed indie documentaries with his college roommate. Felix is unironically proud to be a purveyor of brain rot, constantly bombarding his 942 Instagram followers with clips of new episodes that nobody will watch. It's pathetic and disgusting.

Celeste is a social media coordinator at some nostalgia-bait swimwear line that dropships Walmart-quality bikinis from China. She's trying to launch a brand of functional sea moss supplements, which I've refused to buy multiple times. She's originally from a suburb outside of Atlanta, and took dialect classes to get rid of her Southern accent after graduating from Ole Miss because she thought it would make her more desirable in the fashion industry. Over the past six months, she's lost nearly twenty pounds, mostly in her face and upper thighs, and Sophia is worried she might have some sort of eating disorder, but I'm actually half-hard just looking at her from across the table. She's wearing a three-piece tuxedo from Alexandre Vauthier with a ruffled-collar shirt, black straight-leg pants, and satin Prada pumps.

Felix is wearing last year's Brunello Cucinelli pilot jacket with gray trousers and black Chelsea boots by Saint Laurent. I imagine Felix, scrawny and pale with his Gen Z broccoli haircut, clapping Celeste's cheeks after dinner on his IKEA couch in Los Feliz. I suppress my rage with a large gulp of my Vouvray, and for a brief second, I feel like I might be able to endure the rest of the evening without plunging a knife into my heart. I'm staring at a hand-blown glass installation that's supposed to resemble a cloud when Felix leans forward, speaking with a level of energy that can only be described as methamphetaminic.

"Nathan! My man. How goes the advertising biz? Celeste told me you're a real-life Don Draper out there in Beverly Hills. *Mad Men*, anyone?" he says, glaring at the three of us for approval.

I force a chuckle, the remnants of my somewhat decent mood evaporating.

"They haven't fired me yet, so I must be doing something right."

"Atta boy!" he blurts, as a clump of spittle forms in the crevice of his lips. "You're crushing it, *crushing it*."

He grips the table with his stubby fingers. I nod mechanically as I use my thumb to hunt for loose cuticles. Felix focuses his attention on Sophia, flashes a smile, and it becomes glaringly obvious that he got a veneer job—two rows of comically big porcelain slats.

"And *this* girl—the beautiful birthday girl—future interior design queen of Hollywood! Are you working on any cool projects you can tell us about?"

Sophia eats this up and I zone out while she blabbers about a Spanish Colonial revival in Bel Air, an artists' retreat in Santa Monica, a condo in Brentwood. Before I have a chance to start tearing away a fresh cuticle on my pinky finger, a not-bad-looking waitress approaches our table and explains the nuances of the eight-course tasting menu, which is $570 per person and includes a premium wine pairing.

"I don't think I've ever been this excited for a meal in my *life*," Felix gushes. "Nate—can I call you Nate?—I don't know how you got us in here tonight, but cheers to you, boss man."

Celeste cuts in, the volume of her voice wildly inappropriate.

"But more importantly, cheers to the *birthday giiiirrrllll*!"

After the muted clink of our wine glasses, I take an aggressive gulp of my South African Palomino Fino, barely mustering the willpower not to chug it. After what feels like hours of meaningless drivel about a wedding Celeste attended in Bali, our first course arrives: foamed macadamia milk paired with golden Kaluga caviar and caramelized shallot. Felix takes one bite.

"Oh...*ohmygod*." His eyes roll back into his head, and he makes this audible moaning noise, as if he's having an orgasm. "It should be *illegal* for something to taste this good."

Felix licks his fork not once but twice, like a rabid animal. A table of four MILFs next to us sees this and they start snickering condescendingly. I taste the caviar next and it really is fucking incredible, but Felix's antics are spoiling it for me. To change the topic, I force myself to ask him if he's read anything good recently, hoping this will make him insecure. He squints and clasps his hands in thought. Exhales.

"I'm in the middle of this book called *Feral Symphony* by...I'm blanking on his name."

"Oh my God!" Sophia blurts out, eyes widening. "One of the girls at work just lent me her copy of that!"

"Get out!" Felix smacks the table, causing a waiter across the dining room to glare at us.

"About the queer rat, right?" Sophia asks for confirmation. "I'm dying to read it. It's so short."

"Yeah! Wow, this book is really having a moment. Anyway, Nate, get this: The whole book is narrated by a queer rat living in a New York subway tunnel. The rat can't stand all the finance bros and the girls on an allowance turning the city into a stuffy hellhole. Then the subway gets flooded, so the rat is forced into the streets where it terrorizes a bunch of rich people until they leave. It's basically a parable about oppression and gentrification and how 21st-century America tries to erase people who are already marginalized, especially queer working-class people."

I'm nodding studiously, doing my best not to dissociate, when it registers that *Feral Symphony* is the same book I saw on the PEN/Faulkner shortlist. I'm pretty sure I also skimmed through a long, syrupy feature in the *Los Angeles Times* about the debut author—some waifish Columbia MFA grad who they called "deliriously gifted."

"This book is what fiction *should* be," Felix says, wiping a drop of macadamia milk off of his stubble. "It's inventive and socially conscious, but still super readable."

"I'll add it to my list," I murmur.

"But if you're more of a nonfiction guy, I read—well, I *listened*—to something called *Young Forever* by this functional medicine doctor. I found him on Andrew Huberman's podcast. It's all about, like, reframing how you think about aging. Like getting older doesn't always have to mean *feeling* older, or even getting sick. And he talks about how you can actually eat certain plants as medicine to *age in reverse*. I was so shook. You can keep that beautiful head of hair for the rest of your life!"

I catch Celeste sneaking a glance at my hairline when our second course arrives: Japanese snapper sashimi with micro florals. After our server explains where, how, and why the shaved celtuce was grown, Felix speaks with a mouthful of semi-chewed fish.

"We should totally grab drinks sometime and talk books. I've got so many epic recommendations for you. I'm actually thinking of starting a book club for the boys. Hey, that's some nice alliteration, isn't it? Maybe I should send in an application for a copywriter KBM! Celeste, babe, remind me to give Nate my copy of *Feral Symphony* ASAP after I finish it."

"I wouldn't hold your breath, Nathan," Celeste says sarcastically, nearly spilling her wine. "At the rate Felix reads, you might not get your hands on that book until *Christmas*."

The three of them roar with laughter.

"Bullying is our love language," Felix says, nudging Celeste with his elbow and rolling his eyes.

Sophia clears her throat.

"Well," she says, lowering her voice to create intrigue. "Speaking of books, Nathan's actually writing a novel of his *own*."

My vision narrows, my pulse rises, my forehead heats up. A deep sense of shame, followed by terror, surges through my veins. I'm helpless to stop it. I tear off a piece of skin from my ring finger in search of relief.

"Oh my gosh, I *love* that for you," Celeste blurts out.

Felix's jaw drops.

"Bro, what?! That's *epic*. What's it about? How to get as handsome as you?"

I look down at my half-eaten snapper, forced to reckon with the fact that I haven't written a single fucking word even though I told Sophia and two British skincare influencers at

Tower Bar that I have "the first few chapters in a good place." I refocus my attention, wishing I had at least one more drink in me to lie confidently.

"It's fiction—literary fiction," I add, as if that matters. "It's kind of a satirical take on how the internet impacts youth culture. I'm still outlining the plot, fleshing out the character arcs, stuff like that. But it should be done before the New Year."

Sophia drapes her arm over my shoulder. My blood curdles.

"He's just being humble. It's going to be a *bestseller*."

I want to die—not in a melodramatic, crying-for-help way, but in a sterile, almost clinical fashion. They're looking at me with anticipation, like I'm some kind of rising star on the verge of declaring something profound, which is worse than them thinking I'm a fraud, because now there are expectations. Expectations lead to failure, and failure leads to exposure. A bead of sweat rolls down from my armpit. My knee starts bouncing. I take a sip of lukewarm water to unstick my tongue from the roof of my mouth, stalling as I try to think of something clever or mysterious, but all I see is a blank Google Doc.

"Whatever it is, I want a signed copy," says Felix with a toothy grin.

As the waiter brings out our third course—sea urchin uni egg with champagne butter sauce, green asparagus, and borage blossoms—it becomes harder to deny that I have to publish this novel, or at least finish writing it, to get the upper hand over Felix, socially and professionally. If I don't, I'll become another voice in the chorus of dilettantes floating around LA—one of those angsty, over-educated dreamers who tinkers half-heartedly with their screenplay, their novel, their album until they inevitably succumb to the safety of a monthly paycheck or the family money tree. I fantasize about an elaborate book launch party—maybe at Hotel Bel-Air or Chateau Marmont—with a live reading and a signing ceremony. Hors d'oeuvres, live music, an open bar, a signature cocktail. Felix would give me a pat on the back and pretend to be happy for me. But deep down, he'd be bitterly jealous that I created something completely and uniquely my own as opposed to whatever slop he forces down the gullet of America's sugar-addicted pigs.

I snap myself out of this reverie by reaching to take a bite of my sea urchin uni egg, but realize my ring finger is still bleeding badly, so I wrap it with my napkin. Celeste is talking about a ketamine nasal spray she's trying to get a prescription for. I hate how she finishes all of her sentences with an upward inflection and I wish she would cut her bangs, but decide I'd still fuck her if the opportunity presented itself. I finish my uni, wash it down with the rest of my wine, and excuse myself to use the restroom, realizing my buzz is stronger than I expected.

I wash the blood off my finger, which has congealed into a sort of glue-like consistency. It turns the water in the sink pink. I look at myself in the mirror and tuck back a few stray hairs above my forehead, wondering how many more years my hairline will last. I pat my hands dry and wrap my finger with a Band-Aid. If anyone asks, I'll say I pinched it under a dumbbell at the gym this morning. When I return to my seat, I notice that the waiter has folded my napkin and I'm embarrassed at the thought of her seeing the blood spots all over it. Felix is telling Sophia and Celeste about a lymphatic drainage clinic he just joined in Silver Lake.

"Ideally, your lymphatic system should be able to do all the work on its own. But every day, we're exposed to irritants from processed foods, pollution, stress, all that stuff. Every time your body feels attacked, it tries to protect itself by throwing water, trying to release that inflammation. And you get bloated. Water weight has nothing to do with fat. So what they do is they basically coax excess water and toxins towards the lymph nodes to detox them from the body. And it literally changed my life overnight. The next day, I felt super flexible and more energized. But the weirdest part was that I had to *pee* more."

For the main entree, we have a choice between duck or A5 wagyu with charred eggplant, garlic confit, and *jus de boeuf*. I had my heart set on the duck, but that's what Felix ordered, so I reluctantly settle for the wagyu, even though it costs $40 extra and I just ate the same cut of beef last week at n/naka.

Felix regurgitates a quote from a review of Providence in the *Los Angeles Times* (without citation) about how the tasting menu is "beautifully paced," and I tell him that's an impressive observation. The Japanese couple next to us stands up almost silently and leaves. They didn't speak a word to each other all night. By the time I finish dessert (house-made Ecuadorian dark chocolate with passion fruit and caramel), I'm on the cusp of being drunk, so I mentally forgive Sophia for bringing up my failed attempt at writing a book.

We have a long night ahead of us and there's no way I'll be able to endure it sober, so I order a neat pour of Lagavulin 16. For $44, I can buy a temporary sensation of calm and confidence. I can talk to anybody, accomplish anything.

The alcohol is a sedative to my negative feelings, but it's also an accelerant. I'll wake up tomorrow and the void will be deeper and darker than ever, but right now I don't give a fuck. I'm richer than Felix, my girlfriend is hotter than Celeste, and I'm at a restaurant that normies can't get a reservation at. So I'm going to let myself feel good. While it lasts.

The check lands on the table. Felix pretends like he wants to split it. I shake my head no, scrawl down the tip. I think I give 40 percent. A black BMW is outside waiting for us with hazards on. The driver's Armenian. Mid-5os with a puffy face and nicotine fingers. The interior smells like synthetic sandalwood and something sadder underneath it—cigarettes and Chick-fil-A, maybe. He's blasting the AC and it's freezing in the backseat, but I tolerate it because I'm drunk.

Sophia takes a complimentary stick of peppermint gum from the cupholder and plugs her phone in like she owns the vehicle. As we merge onto The 101, she rests her head on my shoulder, holding my hand in her left hand and her phone in her right hand. Me and her phone—her two favorite things in the whole wide world. She's watching a TikTok about a cam girl who sells her farts in glass jars to desperate men on the internet, which makes her giggle uncontrollably.

Birthday Dinner for Sophia (Continued)

WE PULL OFF The 110 onto 6th Street. I'm comfortably drunk but coming to grips with how many mind-numbing conversations I'm about to endure with raging megalomaniacs. A sense of dread slowly begins to override the alcohol's synthetic tranquility. Some nightmare of a song by Cardi B and Megan Thee Stallion is blasting in our Uber XL (Sophia must have connected her phone to the SUV's Bluetooth) and she timed it so her favorite part would play as she hoisted herself out of the BMW: *Gotta garage full of foreign cars that I never drove / A bitch couldn't school me with a student loan.*

Celeste made reservations for the four of us and a carefully selected group of Sophia's friends at Spire 73, a rooftop lounge on the 73rd floor of the InterContinental Los Angeles Downtown. At 1,100 feet, it's the tallest open-air bar in the Western hemisphere. Outside the entrance, there's a pregnant homeless woman clutching a dirty Styrofoam cup from 7-Eleven. In her other hand, she's clinging to a damp cardboard square with a faded message scrawled in Sharpie, but between the illegible handwriting and my slightly blurred vision, I can't make out what it says—something about cancer and jobs.

We file into the elevator with three blandly attractive blonde women in their early twenties. They stare at their phones, tap indiscriminately, and smack gum. One of them has to keep pulling her minidress down because it's riding up her ass. My eyes are drawn to her soft, supple cheeks like magnets, and I can feel myself getting semi-hard, so I subtly tuck my dick behind the waist of my John Varvatos trousers.

We step onto the rooftop, which is encased by heavy-duty glass to protect us from the cold winds and ensure nobody falls or jumps to their death on the pavement below. I look out into the night sky, which is defaced by a giant, glowing red logo of a management consulting company on the building across from us. I shift my gaze downward and see The 10, The 101, and The 110—all glowing with trails of red and white lights, writing an endless message in some awful, unreadable language.

Sophia's girlfriends—an indistinguishable mass of self-tanning serum and lip filler—shriek when they see her. They hug and peck each other on the cheek and whisper and squeal and take duck-face selfies and immediately retake them. I can't decide whether I'm more infuriated by their joy or my own anger. While she's preoccupied, I wander to the bar, desperate to preserve my buzz, and order something with mezcal, St. Germaine, and Aperol that costs $27. I finish it in four gulps before telling a bartender who has the dead eyes of a failed actor to keep the tab open. While pretending to study the cocktail menu, I see Sophia out of the corner of my eye, hurtling towards me.

"Hey, mister! You disappeared," she says, nearly tripping over herself.

"I figured I'd let you...socialize," I say absently.

"Can we take some pictures together, pretty please?" she pleads, tugging on the sleeve of my fatigue jacket. "I basically starved myself for six weeks to fit into this skirt and I need evidence to prove it to my sister."

Turning down Sophia's request for pictures will create more problems than it solves, not to mention sex will be out of the question later, so I reluctantly agree to play the role of supportive boyfriend. As I slide down from the barstool, I feel my eyes drooping and notice that I'm starting to lose sensation in my extremities. I'm slurring answers to her friends' questions—about the caviar at Providence, about the new KHAITE suede hobo bag I bought Sophia, about why I'm not smiling—and I'm unsure of the words that I let ooze out of my mouth. They cackle, either at me or with me. I can't tell and I refuse to care. I piece together fragments like "slay" and "iconic" and "giving *Vogue*." But then something stands out amongst the racket.

"Smile, Mr. Future Author!" I hear a female with a distinct Valley accent shout as I'm momentarily blinded by the white flash of an iPhone camera. I blink, dazed, and try to recalibrate. I can't tell whether I'm being mocked or worshiped. But the bigger issue is that Sophia has been running her mouth about my novel, and the news is spreading faster than I can do damage control. The problem isn't that I haven't written a single sentence; it's that I don't have an *idea*, a concept, that I can impress anyone with. You can coast along for months or even years making vague declarations about some nonexistent creative project and be taken semi-seriously if you string together a few coherent sentences. But stammering as I try to articulate a basic plotline will be social suicide.

"So, like, what is your book about?" I hear the Valley voice ask again. The upward inflection, the vocal fry, and the overuse of filler words make me nauseous. But as my gaze refocuses, I see that the Valley voice comes from Kendal

Behkar, Sophia's assistant at Manuel-Ballard. She's a petite 23-year-old Persian with a severe, dark beauty: olive skin, almond-shaped eyes, high-arched eyebrows, an expensive nose job, strong cheekbones, plump lips, and a perfect set of tits with full cleavage on display. We met a few months ago at a dinner party that Sophia's boss hosted in the Bird Streets, and there was a vague sexual tension when Kendal cornered me by the hors d'oeuvres and insisted that I looked like Henry Cavill.

"Are you gonna write about *Sophia?*" she asks in a borderline seductive tone—a bold move given Sophia is within earshot. I instinctively reach for my drink, trying to play off my sudden onset horniness, but quickly realize I don't have one.

"That's...something you'll have to see for yourself," I slur, trying to play it cool.

"So mysterious," she says in a honey-smooth voice. "Very writer-ly of you."

Unable to formulate a coherent response, I force a chuckle, making a valiant effort to prevent my eyes from drifting towards her chest. Sophia slips out from a swarm of girls beside us, nestling herself up against me. The sparkle in Kendal's eyes dies out.

"He won't let me read a *word* of his book," Sophia says in a mock-complaining voice. "He's so protective of this work, just like he is about me, right, babe?"

"You took the words right out of my mouth," I reply, trying not to sound completely deflated.

After posing for at least 75 pictures (we had to take them on iPhone with and without flash, then on film) I stumble back to the bar where a server offers me a blanket. I decline but hand him a crisp $50 bill anyway. A Latina woman next to me wearing an oversized blazer with nothing but a bra underneath keeps bragging to her less attractive friend that she can finally drunk drive because she has Full Self-Driving on her Tesla and for some reason she asks what I do and I tell her I get paid a stupid amount of money to come up with ideas to sell shit like toothpaste and laundry detergent. She laughs and her voice buzzes lightly in my head but it doesn't register since she brushes something nonexistent off my shoulder. She flips a lock of thick caramel brown hair behind her ear and I catch a whiff of Guerlain Tobacco Honey and I come dangerously close to suggesting we Uber back to my place and fuck each other's brains out. But I restrain myself, slurring something about how I'm here for "a friend's" birthday party before ordering a bottle of Veuve Clicquot Brut Rosé. It was intended for Sophia, but I end up drinking half of it, so I order another.

It's almost 1 a.m. and I'm craving sugar so I order chocolate truffle cake and a platter of s'mores. I'm feeding a spoonful to Sophia while her friend Chloe, a hollow-eyed redhead, keeps rifling through a green Bulgari purse, apparently looking for her last Vicodin which she misplaced. She has a small, fine-line tattoo on the inside of her forearm that says "HANDLE WITH CARE." According to Sophia, I met Chloe at a charity event at the West Hollywood EDITION for an organization focused on ocean conservation.

"Oh yeah, of course," I say, even though I have no idea who she is. "Such a sweetheart."

While they start talking about one of their girlfriends who cheated on her fiancée with some guy on the Clippers, I excuse myself to go throw up in the bathroom but accidentally wander into the women's restroom where a woman with stenciled-on eyebrows shoves me out. I stumble into a stall in the men's room, collapse to my knees, jam my mutilated index finger down my throat, and heave. My vomit is ruby red because of the wine I drank at Providence and I can see chunks of golden Kaluga caviar and micro florals—a $570 meal floating in the toilet. As I stare at my vomit, its acrid odor wafting upward from the toilet, I tell myself tomorrow is the day I start writing.

I trudge back out to the blurry terrace where "Borderline" by Tame Impala is playing. I mumble along to the lyrics, oblivious to where anyone is or whether they can hear me. I spend the rest of the night sauntering aimlessly around the bar before some irate manager tells us to leave around 2:30. I drift in and out of consciousness in the back seat of an Escalade that I don't remember calling.

All of a sudden I'm in Sophia's bed and it registers that I'm supposed to have sex with her, but my dick only gets half-hard so I just go down on her, aimlessly and lazily lapping at and around her clit, until I fall asleep naked on the cold, linen sheets.

Wasting Time at Sophia's

I WAKE UP IN THE DARKNESS, freezing, and roll over in a panic to check my phone—5:48 a.m. My mouth is dry and tastes like battery acid, my stomach is convulsing, my head is pounding from sugar, salt, alcohol, and sleep deprivation. Despite the damage, I have a throbbing erection, which quickly deflates as I'm engulfed by an overwhelming sense of dread and anxiety over what I might have said or done last night.

I force myself to replay the events of the night: Did Kendal Behkar catch me staring at her tits? What did I tell Sophia's friends about my novel? Who took pictures of me? Where are those pictures now? Everything blurs together into an ugly montage of noise and half-smiles. The effort it takes to parse through the memories aggravates my headache so I shut my eyes and try to force myself back to sleep but it makes me nauseous so I just stare at the blank white ceiling until the urge to piss is stronger than my hangxiety.

I swivel out of the bed, careful not to wake Sophia who won't be up for at least another two, maybe three hours. I almost step on her dog, Coco, the purebred Pomeranian she bought from a breeder in Ojai a few months ago. I hate this dog because it makes repulsive, high-pitched yapping noises, routinely pisses inside, and has made a habit of chewing my shoes—behaviors that could have easily been corrected by paying for basic training, which Sophia didn't feel was necessary because she found her own training videos on TikTok. I rifle through a mound of linen sheets to find my

Calvin Klein boxer briefs and slip into them before shuffling into the bathroom as blood rushes either into or out of my head. I can't tell which.

The bathroom is sterile, borderline clinical—a gray tile floor, chrome fixtures, harsh fluorescent lights that make every pore, crease, and imperfection glaringly obvious. I'm too disgusted to look at myself in the mirror so I lurch to the toilet, balancing myself with one hand on the wall, and piss for what seems like a full minute. My urine is dark amber, almost brown. I tally the obscene amount of wine, champagne, and mezcal I needed to drink to get through last night and nearly gag into the toilet. I try to swallow but my tongue is stuck to the roof of my mouth like Velcro. I sidestep to the sink and turn the faucet on, noticing the dried blood around the nail bed of my ring finger. I cup the ice-cold water in my hands and splash my face, a futile gesture to wash away the sour shame.

I walk past the bedroom where Coco has taken my spot on the bed and wander into the kitchen, which is dark, bitterly cold, and follows the template of every other "modern luxury" apartment kitchen you'll find in this city: vinyl plank flooring, particle board cabinets, fake quartz countertops, stainless steel appliances—all the veneers of opulence without any of the substance. A shrine to mediocrity.

I open the refrigerator and rummage through colorful rows of Pressed juices, Celsius energy drinks, and meal-prepped chicken until I find a bottle of Mountain Valley Spring Water. I chug it and feel the cool liquid revive me as it works its way through my intestines. I grab another bottle and chug half. I should go back to bed and rest, but the odds are high that Sophia will attempt to cuddle. I'm not remotely in

64

the mood to tolerate that, so I slump onto the green faux velvet sofa in her living room and stare out onto Laurel Avenue.

The street is lifeless except for a homeless man, hunch-backed, sunburnt to a crisp, and barefoot, pushing a Ralphs shopping cart full of crushed aluminum cans and empty plastic bottles. He tries to cross the street onto Fountain Avenue, but somehow misses a step, causing the cart to tumble over the curb. All of the cans and bottles spill onto the pavement, rolling in different directions. Two construction workers in a dirt-caked pickup truck swerve around the pile of plastic and aluminum, leaving the man in a cloud of black exhaust while he strains to pick his items up, placing them one by one back into the cart.

To distract myself from the menacing silence, I inspect Sophia's bookshelf, a kaleidoscope of bright, glossy spines stacked in alternating orientations. It's more curation than collection, conspicuously devoid of literature. The books are just for decoration—*objets d'art* is the term she uses. There are oversized hardcovers that highlight the works of Rothko, Hockney, Matisse, and Basquiat. There are fashion books about Dior, Chanel, Alexander McQueen, and Tom Ford. There's a book of vintage Santa Barbara photography. There's a book that consists entirely of *Vogue* covers. There's one that's just called *Cabins*. No well-thumbed novels, no dog-eared pages, no dusty biographies. The hardcover edition of *Glamorama* that I bought for Sophia at Book Soup when we first started dating sits untouched, propped up against *The Little Book of Hermes*.

The only book I see with a creased spine is *Feral Symphony*, which, from what I remember during last night's dinner, was lent to Sophia by her coworker at Manuel-Ballard.

I pull it off the shelf to see who I'm competing against in the world of literary fiction. The cover is magenta with the title scrawled in all caps with what's supposed to look like black crayon. Directly below: Martin DuVall. In the middle of the cover is a sketch of a grayish-brown rat staring menacingly into the distance with 'A NOVEL' stamped across the length of its pink tail. In the upper right-hand corner, there's a PEN/FAULKNER Finalist badge. For some reason, I assumed it would be painfully overwritten, but it's slim and light. More brochure than book. I fan the pages with my thumb — 14-point font, unnecessarily frequent line breaks — and stop at the end to see the page count: 119. I flip it over to look at the back cover, which has a blurb from *The New York Times* centered at the top:

"DuVall has crafted a fever dream of a novel that bears witness to gentrification, climate change, gender identity, and political unrest through the lens of the least expected character: a subway rat. Compassionate, fierce, and seductively original, *Feral Symphony* is an act of spellbinding imagination that anyone with a conscience needs to read."

I was zoning in and out of focus when Felix attempted to articulate the plot at dinner last night, so I scan the synopsis to jog my memory:

"A queer, destitute rat struggles to assert their existence in a disease-ridden subway tunnel beneath the bustling metropolis of Manhattan. Infuriated by finance bros and nepo babies invading their native land, our lonely narrator spends their days rummaging for food scraps, listening to commuters whine about first world problems, and grappling with the complexities of their gender identity, the indignities of gentrification, looming climate catastrophes..."

I trail off and read three more blurbs at the bottom of the back cover:

"This gem of a novel oozes wisdom, page after ravishing page" — *The Washington Post*

"Finally, the book America deserves" — *Vanity Fair*

"DuVall joins the ranks of luminaries like George Orwell and James Baldwin, with a dash of Joan Didion...nothing short of a prophet" — *The San Francisco Chronicle*

I can't say that I know what genuine inspiration feels like. But I imagine this is the closest I'll get. Not because I want to write my own pseudo-intellectual fairy tale that someone can breeze through on a three-hour flight. But because if something this shallow—a few thousand buzzwords duct-taped into a story—can be a critic's wet dream, anything I eventually write should catapult me into literary stardom. It's like finding out all you have to do to win a Grammy is hit a button on your keyboard to play a preset song.

I make a mental note to channel this energy into my next writing session, then sprawl out on the sofa. As I brush away a clump of Coco's fur, I think back to the first night I spent here last spring. Sophia and I had been out on two dates—drinks at Death & Co and dinner at La Dolce Vita— after we met at an album release party for a German pop/soul ensemble in Mount Olympus, and she quickly became obsessed with me. Her exact words were "It scares me how fascinated I am by you" (a line she later said she was embarrassed to say, but admitted was ultimately true).

The most action I got from Sophia on the first two dates was a quick squeeze of her ass while we made out at a valet stand because she wanted me to "play my cards right." Thankfully, for our third date, she invited me to her apartment, where she cooked spicy vodka rigatoni (edible, although the sauce was a little runny). We got drunk off of a couple bottles of 2014 Foradori Nosiola that were collecting dust in my kitchen, after which I put on a "stellar performance" (her words) on the green velvet sofa. Over the next couple of months, we got dragged to birthday parties for losers we barely knew, wasted money on unimaginative food at overrated restaurants, and went to a gallery opening for an artist whose paintings were so banal that I actually emailed the curator to let her know how embarrassed she should be.

We lied to each other about how happy we were with the trajectory of our lives. We went to farmers' markets and bought organic mangoes that rotted in Sophia's kitchen. We booked a vineyard tour in Sonoma, where I met her parents who said I "seemed like a really great guy."

I thought I'd match Sophia's passion as the weeks snowballed into months. Instead, I've lapsed into terminal boredom. Once the novelty of the sex wore off, I started noticing things I hated about Sophia. How she made me take my shoes off in her apartment but let her dog with shit-streaked paws climb into bed with us; the agonizing sound of her acrylic nails clacking on her phone screen when she types; the way she skips to the next song in a playlist with only a few seconds left instead of finishing it; how she randomly slips into an ironic British accent and waits for me to laugh.

I'm still seeing Sophia because she's probably the most attractive woman I can fuck, but also because the relationship keeps me insulated from myself. I don't have to reflect or evolve or have any kind of personal reckonings—because she doesn't want to either. The numbing inertia of our relationship is addictive, but I've thought about ending it multiple times—either directly or by sabotaging it to the point that she'd be forced to dump me. But I end up convincing myself that keeping a stale relationship on life support is more tolerable than putting myself through the hell of dating someone new.

The past six weeks were particularly bleak, which is why I cheated on her with a Brazilian medical student I met at my cousin's wedding in Santorini, a travel influencer I DMd on Instagram, a waitress at Horses (I only got a blowjob because she was on her period), and my pool mistress, Lana.

I'm not proud of myself for cheating. Most of the time it's not even worth the hassle. But the window of time between flirting and climaxing gives me a potent hit of validation, of being needed, and that's apparently enough for me. The women are a sedative to my misery as well as an accelerant, like a glass of Macallan 14.

My temples throb, snapping me back into focus. I drink the rest of the Mountain Valley water while Coco stares at me in the doorway with her head cocked and her tongue drooping. I want to punt her across the room—either that or stuff her in the freezer. I look back out the window and see the homeless man has replaced all of the cans and bottles into his shopping cart and is back to pushing it down Fountain. He'll probably make around ten dollars today off his litter.

There's nothing else to do, so I saunter back to the bedroom. Sophia has a half-moon-shaped vanity mirror instead of a headboard, so I avoid looking at myself when I climb into bed. She's curled up into a little ball, sleeping peacefully, and for some reason, this irritates me. I glare at the ceiling and wait for a thought that never arrives, and soon the emptiness is filled by hate — hate toward myself for pretending to be interested in other people's pointless lives, hate toward Felix for being a dopamine-chasing pseudo-intellectual, hate toward KBM and Krause's nephew who thinks he can waltz into the agency without merit, hate toward my parents for the platinum shackles they put me in as soon as I was born.

I try to make a mental sketch of a life that isn't plagued by a terrible emptiness and boredom, but it's too much work so I reach for my phone and check the time — 6:19. Sophia is supposed to drive me home, but she's showing no signs of waking up any time soon, so I roll over and start watching a video on mute of a man who pays an assassin to try to kill him.

Chapter One

IT'S SUNDAY NIGHT and I'm still fighting off the residue of my hangover, but my boredom is unbearable so I sit down at my Jean Prouvé desk to start my career as a novelist. I turn on my iMac—24-inch 4.5K Retina display, studio-quality microphone, six-speaker sound system. The screen is only 11.5 millimeters thick, which is made possible by Apple's new M1 chip that integrates the processor, graphics, and memory onto a single tiny piece of silicon. I want to listen to music while I write because I read somewhere that it drowns out your subconscious thoughts, so I put on my Space Gray AirPods Max headphones. They have personalized Spatial Audio with dynamic head tracking, Active Noise Cancellation mode, Transparency mode, and up to 20 hours of listening time. As soon as they sync with my iMac, a wave of hope rushes over me. I'm ready to lock in.

But first, I Google "best music for focus." An article in *Entrepreneur*, written by a neuroscientist, explains that classical music has been proven to "stimulate neural connections that improve concentration, memory, and creativity" (the absence of words in the music is the main factor, as songs that contain lyrics have been found to be a distraction when you're trying to focus). I type "classical" into the search bar of Apple Music and choose Chopin's Nocturnes. "Chopin's nocturnes could well have been written for the voice," notes Apple Music's editorial staff. "Their beautiful, lyrical melodies unfold with a magic that few composers for piano can match." I give myself a nod of approval before shuffling the collection. The first work is *Op. 9 No. 1 in B-Flat Minor*. It sounds good enough to me, so I minimize that tab and open a new Google Doc.

I stare into the blank white screen and I can physically feel the hope mutate into terror at the thought of trying to fill this entire page and the next one and the one after that. The tiny black cursor in the top left corner blinks and reminds me of someone tapping their finger, daring me to say something, to scream into the hellish void.

I try to recall the half-baked idea that I mentioned at dinner last night—something about a teenage fame addict in the Valley. He's an isolated, socially inept underachiever whose idea of success lies in accumulating the most valuable currency of our time: fame. The celebrities he's obsessed with aren't actors or musicians or athletes, but garden variety teenagers who make millions of dollars by filming themselves doing inane horseshit and uploading it for an equally dull audience that needs slop to distract them from the bleak horror of everyday life. And this character of my creation is hell bent on replicating that blueprint, pixel for pixel. I imagine the kid filming himself pulling pranks on innocent bystanders at shopping malls, public parks, and concerts. He's filming on an iPhone, so the video quality isn't exactly cinematic. He doesn't have much confidence on camera. He obsesses over algorithms, thumbnails, titles, engagement metrics, comments, and clips. He gets a few hundred views a week, mostly from classmates watching ironically. But the handful of true fans he accumulates urge him to push legal and ethical boundaries. By the time summer break rolls around, he's a slave to the demands of a few dozen teenagers, committing (and filming) increasingly horrific acts to himself and others—I'm imagining violence, sexual deviance, desecration of sacred property.

Maybe this kid suffers a life-altering injury. Maybe he livestreams a felony, gets arrested, tried as an adult, and sent to prison. Maybe he gets everything he wanted, but ends up hanging himself with an extension cord in his parents' garage. The climax of the story is less important than the premise, which is to lay bare the chilling nihilism and the eager pursuit of mediocrity that defines our rotting corpse of an empire. I don't have an outline or plot summary or character descriptions or research documents. I don't have any formal writing training, other than the composition classes I took in college. I refuse to join any loser-magnet writing workshops or read how-to books about the art of storytelling or, God forbid, enroll in an MFA program. My ideas, my taste, my opinions, and my intuition will give me enough fuel to produce a respectable novel. I believe I can white-knuckle my way to the words on the screen matching what's in my head

I rest my fingertips on the middle row of my Apple Magic Keyboard. It has an extended layout with document navigation controls, a scissor mechanism beneath each key for increased stability, optimized key travel, and a low profile for a more precise typing experience. I don't know how to start, so my fingertips just rest on the keys and suddenly they feel really cold. The page is blank. The cursor is blinking.

After maybe three minutes, I anxiously open the iMessage app on my computer, desperate for a distraction. The only message I have is from Sophia—she bought a purple toothpaste serum to get rid of some imaginary yellow stains she has. I don't respond. I'm six minutes into Chopin's Nocturnes and I decide to switch to Bach's Cello Suites. The sound of cello is more relaxing than the sound of piano, and I hopelessly tell myself this will elevate my level of focus. Instead of forcing words onto the screen, I'm trying to decide whether to narrate the story in first or third person. Most of my favorite novels are autofiction and I imagine writing in the first person requires less effort. My decision is made. The page is blank, the cursor is blinking, the Cello Suites play in the background. I imagine my main character, a 16-year-old, scrolling mindlessly on his phone during a European history class. He's fantasizing about amassing millions of followers and landing lucrative brand sponsorship deals and driving a blue Lamborghini down the 405. I type 82 words and read them back to myself. I hate all of it, so I select all the text with my cursor and sheepishly press "delete."

By now, I'm tense and irritable and even though I poisoned my body last night, I walk to the kitchen to pour myself a glass of Macallan 18 to tranquilize myself. I drink it neat out of a crystal Glencairn Glass, which has a tapered mouth to capture and focus the scotch's aroma on the nose. After four sips I feel my mind loosen and my jaw relax. I bring the scotch back to my desk, placing it next to the D.S. & Durga candle that Sophia bought me for an occasion I can't remember. The page is still blank. The cursor is still blinking. I increase the font size and type "Chapter 1" at the top of the page. The default Arial font in my Google Doc looks too informal, so I change it between Georgia and EB Garamond before finally settling on Times New Roman. That looks too academic, so I change it again to Georgia.

I type a sentence describing a high school classroom. It's too vague, so I delete it.

I type a sentence describing how bored the character is during class. It's too pretentious, so I delete it.

I type a sentence about a viral prank video that inspires the character to attempt his own. I think I can build on this. I type another sentence and another. The words don't flow, they plop out like turds out of a dog's ass, some faster than others. I glance at the time, and it's been 53 minutes since I first sat down. I check my word count: 96. Not even enough for a screenshot to post on Instagram. The arbitrary goal I set for myself was 500, but my eyes are feeling a little dry so I save the document as "Chapter 1" and shut down the iMac.

I walk to the kitchen, pour another Macallan, and take the elevator up to the rooftop, where I plan to snoop on some Instagram models until my frustration fades back into my subconscious. When the elevator doors open, I look out toward the terrace and see Lana, curled up in a powder blue Alo hoodie, sipping a tumbler of white wine next to the outdoor fireplace, her face illuminated by the flickering blue light of her phone. We lock eyes. My pulse rises and my dick jumps inside my Calvin Klein briefs. She flashes a soft, seductive smile, almost as if she was expecting me. She knows exactly what she's doing, and so do I.

"Look who it is," she says, swirling her wine. "My favorite author."

We skip the small talk.

Shrink

DR. ALPER ASKS if I've been using the Cognitive Restructuring worksheet he gave me after our last session. I lie and assure him I use it religiously, especially when I feel like blocking my parents' phone numbers or trying to fuck Sophia's friends. He nods and there's no chance he believes me, but we have to move on because the clock is ticking and I was late since Maru Espresso Bar only had one brain-dead barista working.

Most of these sessions consist of aching boredom punctuated by long, awkward silences. Dr. Alper probably hates me since I don't crawl into his office every week without a clue, desperate to swallow empty platitudes. I want him to know I'm of a different caliber than his roster of soft-brained, TikTok-educated patients. But more importantly, I want him to know I'm at least as smart as he is, if not smarter. And so rather than surrender to Dr. Alper and let him take a scalpel to my tangled thought patterns, I end up fencing with him, deflecting and dodging Wednesday after Wednesday, hoping he'll eventually admit that I should just keep living the way I want to because he doesn't have the prowess to fix me.

While Dr. Alper is on a tangent about the physical symptoms of stress, my mind wanders to a story I read this morning about a 14-year-old girl in a Chicago suburb who killed herself after two weeks of virtual therapy with a chatbot powered by artificial intelligence. She took an entire bottle of her mom's Oxycodone before the family's nanny found her on the bathroom floor with a deep gash on her forehead.

"How have you been spending your free time recently?" Dr. Alper asks, steering the conversation. I crane my neck to figure out what kind of watch he's wearing—a Rolex Oyster Perpetual, maybe—but his arms are crossed over a black wool turtleneck, so I can't tell. It's suddenly freezing in here. I chew the inside of my cheek with my canines, thinking carefully of what to say. I decide to throw Dr. Alper a bone and mention my book, careful to portray it as an act of organic creative expression, not desperation.

"I've been trying to...write," I say with a cool, steady gaze.

Dr. Alper crosses his legs slowly.

"You didn't tell me you were a writer," he says in a distant, sort of informal manner.

"I'm not," I mumble, biting a chunk out of my inner lip.

"Last time I checked, a writer is someone who writes," he says, gesturing to a leather-bound Oxford English Dictionary with his glasses. This snarky quip makes me want to bash his wrinkly, cue-ball head through the window.

"The operative word is 'trying,'" I blurt.

"Semantics," he says, gently swatting the air. "What are you *working on?* Can we frame it that way?"

"It's a book—a novel."

"Do you want to tell me what it's about?"

"Not really."

My eye twitches.

"Have you always wanted to be an author?"

"No."

"Why now?"

"Who are you, Charlie Rose?"

"I'm surprised a guy your age knows who Charlie Rose is."

I crack my knuckles, one by one, starting with my index finger and working my way towards the pinky. I do some quick mental math and calculate that my parents are spending $12 per minute, 20 cents per second, for me to sit here making chit-chat about Charlie Rose to reduce the likelihood that I off myself.

"Wasn't it you who had the brilliant idea for me to 'carve out an identity?' Prove to myself that I can 'step out of my family's shadow?'" I ask, making condescending air quotes.

Dr. Alper nods, slightly intrigued, and writes something on his yellow legal pad for 15 seconds. Three dollars.

Fighting Urge to Jack Off at Work

ON THE WAY TO THE OFFICE I'm half-listening to an interview with a neuroscientist from M.I.T. about optimizing your sleep routine. He recommends sleeping next to a red light to stimulate melatonin production, taping your mouth shut to encourage nasal breathing, using organic linen sheets to correct hormone imbalances, and taking a supplement stack that consists of magnesium glycinate, L-theanine, phosphatidylserine, and a quinton isotonic solution. At a stoplight on Gregory, I glance out my window and see a blacked-out G-Wagon parked in a handicap spot outside an urgent care clinic offering free STD tests. I look out the other window and see a billboard that reads "SYPHILIS IS SERIOUS" in blurred white letters over a pair of bloodshot eyes.

As I inch forward on Wilshire, I mindlessly rub my index finger over my thumb until I find a loose cuticle. I dig the nail of my index finger under the cuticle until it comes loose, then tear it away using my opposite index finger and thumb. I feel a drop of cool blood pooling up along my nail bed. I reach for a Band-Aid in my pocket, but the light turns green so I hold my wounded hand in the air, making sure no blood gets on the leather seats of my Porsche Cayenne Turbo GT which are, ironically, blood red.

The Porsche goes from zero to 60 in just over three seconds and can reach a top speed of 189 miles per hour, making it the fastest SUV on the planet. My parents bought me the Porsche after I got promoted to Executive Creative Director at KBM—a noteworthy upgrade from my BMW M4 coupe, which I had actually been paying for out of my own pocket. I haven't told anyone that my parents are footing the $3,050 monthly payment. The only thing that matters is that I'm perceived as someone who belongs in the driver's seat of this vehicle, someone who *earned* it. The novelty of the Porsche wore off after a few months since I can rarely drive faster than 40 miles per hour in LA traffic. And although I can't say it makes me happy, per se, I'd be mortified if I pulled up to the valet at Nobu in a Toyota or even an Audi. So I guess a more accurate assessment is that the Porsche *prevents me from being unhappy*.

On the podcast, the M.I.T. neuroscientist (who's making a pathetic attempt at shilling some book that was ghostwritten for him) says the optimal sleep temperature is 67 degrees and you shouldn't eat, exercise, or look at a screen for at least three hours before going to bed. I'm not interested in this interview in any meaningful way. But if I stop long enough to really think about what I'm doing with my life and how much time I've wasted, if I think about how lost I feel every second of every day, how completely and utterly fucking lost I am, I'll accelerate my Porsche to 189 miles per hour, drive head-on into one of the perfectly manicured palm trees on Santa Monica, and put a clean end to it all.

I pull up to my office building, hand my key to the valet, stand silently in the elevator while I wrap my bloody thumb with a Band-Aid, and prepare for another day as the Executive Creative Director at KBM. It's a little after nine in the morning, and I'm sitting tensely in a purple velvet swivel chair inside a glass box conference room, desperately wishing it was socially acceptable to slug a Bloody Mary. Across from me, there's a guy who I've never seen or spoken to, but all it takes is one look to know he's worthless. He has short, curly hair (must be a Great Clips chop job) and his face is covered in pockmarks. He's wearing a cheap navy blue bomber jacket (H&M or Zara), a pathetic white t-shirt, a pair of Levi's, and clear-framed plastic glasses. He's prattling on about some hike he did in Malibu State Park this weekend—the precise elevation of the summit, the boots he wore, the views of the ocean, the plants, the rocks, the wind. He's telling us how many miles per hour the fucking wind was blowing and in which direction. There are several other tired faces in the conference room, none of whom are even looking at him at this point.

Brooke mercifully starts the meeting and introduces the new loser: Will. They hired him as an Assistant Account Manager yesterday, which means he's a glorified intern with a $75,000 annual salary and a decent benefits package. He'll quit within two years to take a job in-house at some soulless CPG brand where he can hide in a bloated marketing department and make a couple thousand dollars more every year to push paper and exchange emails with other agencies like this one and get married and become house poor and never bother realize how much of a miserable slave he is.

Brooke insists that we're running out of time to come up with campaign ideas we can pitch to the Toothpaste Conglomerate, which hasn't crossed my mind since our meeting last week. She says it's "non-negotiable" that we have at least three viable concepts by the end of this week. She yanks out her MacBook Air along with a monstrous stack of papers covered with Post-it notes that I've never seen or touched. I can tell she's overwhelmed because of the way she crinkles her brow and purses her lips and bobs her left foot up and down underneath the table at a feverish pace.

Most days, Brooke's hysteria makes me want to fling myself out of the 16th-floor window, splattering myself on the pavement of Wilshire. But there are rare moments like today when her neurotic episodes ignite a primal lust that I don't feel around conventionally hot women. Something about her vulnerability, her neediness, her ache for validation, makes me want to pin her up against the whiteboard and fuck the tension out of her. I imagine the unflattering fluorescent lights in the conference room illuminating the glaring imperfections that I'd normally find repugnant but suddenly seem hot: frizzy hair pulled into a sad bun, stretch-marked boobs that are too far apart, thin lips, clumpy mascara. I fetishize all of it to the point that I almost excuse myself to jack off in the bathroom. No organic lube or 4K porn, just the disposable image of this twisted sex symbol I've built up in my head over half a decade. I'm disgusted with myself, but the more I resist the fantasy the more intense it becomes—like being lured to a drive-thru when you've secured a reservation at Somni.

I had a window to make it happen a couple of months ago. We were standing outside Dan Tana's after dinner with the executive team from a grotesque but wildly profitable gin brand. I was sloppy drunk since dirty gin martinis were the only acceptable beverage to consume over three hours. Brooke and I were the last two people at the valet and she kept brushing up against my arm while she fussed about getting ghosted by an egomaniacal accountant at Disney she met on Bumble. They were supposed to watch *Vanilla Sky* (a staple in the Softboy Criterion Collection) at his apartment in Culver City, but he went radio silent for 48 hours.

"Childish and bad taste," I said. "What exactly are you missing out on?"

"I don't know," she whined. "Are LA guys always this horrible, or is it me?"

"Why don't you come back to my place and I'll give you a definitive answer," I said, my voice all laziness and arrogance, leaning my head back against the white brick chimney.

She checked her phone, stalling. No missed calls, unread texts, or Bumble notifications. Just the lock screen photo of the stupid cockapoo she and her roommate adopted.

"It's late," she said sheepishly.

"It's ten," I shot back, keeping my eyes locked on hers as my vision went in and out of focus.

"I..." she stammered as her face flushed beet red. "I wouldn't be able to look Sophia in the eyes at the Clio after-party next weekend."

Her dinged-up Hyundai Sonata pulled up and she scurried toward it, clearly rattled.

"I don't think you would either," I said with a smirk, as if to acknowledge how badly she wanted it.

I snap back to the present, tearing myself away from the fantasy. I pull a few campaign concepts out of my ass for the Toothpaste Conglomerate. Brooke gushed over my "Smile Equity" stunt idea, where we'd bribe a bunch of dentists to set up free clinics in shitty neighborhoods and film a harrowing documentary about it.

I spend the rest of the day deleting emails (47), shopping online for a new suede jacket (I like the Italian goat suede one from Officine Générale), eating lunch at Crustacean by myself (steamed line-caught Chilean sea bass), and Googling inspiration for author photographs to go on the dust jacket of my novel.

Pool

PULLING INTO THE PARKING GARAGE beneath my building, it strikes me that I'm in a decent mood for the first time in weeks. Maybe months. The sea bass at Crustacean was perfectly flaky, the campaign for the Toothpaste Conglomerate is off my plate for at least a week, and Sophia hasn't texted or called since last night. I check the clock on the Porsche's dashboard: 3:27. I sit in the car with the AC running, debating whether to spend this block of the afternoon hammering out the rest of Chapter One, but the horniness I fought off at the office swells up inside me again. It's 74 and sunny, which means there's a good chance Lana is oiling herself up at the pool. I rush upstairs and change into my new Stone Island swim shorts and rehearse a few conversation starters in the mirror:

I think you wasted your money buying a book that tells you how to "do nothing"—it looks like you've mastered that art.

Have you tried L'Éclat, the new French restaurant on Melrose? So overrated. (I haven't been).

Are you planning to even out that tan line with sunlight or Facetune?

The pool deck is baking underneath an immense, bleached sky. The smell of coconut sunscreen, chlorine, and body oil hangs in the heat. I take inventory of the languid bodies sprawled about. An emaciated man (probably an ex-model) with silver fingernails in a pair of white briefs that say "FUCK ME" in arched, blue letters across his buttocks. A Persian woman with a pair of surgically aspirational tits that don't move, scrolling on her phone with mechanical disinterest. A heavily tattooed Korean woman with platinum hair doing what looks like some kind of breathwork ritual under one of the cabanas. The closest person to me is a woman in her late thirties, who I see tanning up here year-round. I've never seen her so much as dip her toe into the water, no matter how hot it gets. Her body is phenomenal (for her age), but I can't make an accurate assessment of her overall attractiveness because she's wearing oversized Dior sunglasses that cover half her face. She's been reading *The Creative Act* by Rick Rubin for three months.

I scan the windows of the units overlooking the pool— I see a girl with blonde pigtails, no older than 23, recording herself with a ring light clamped to her iPhone. She does that thing with her head where she tilts it like she's hearing a secret, grins into the void, does a little shoulder dance. She stops, repositions, smiles again. A loop.

Roy Ayers plays over the Bose speakers bolted to the concrete walls.

My life, my life, my life, my life in the sunshine
Everybody loves the sunshine

Lana's absence starts to feel personal. But I've already committed to spending the rest of the day up here, so I sink into a lounge chair and pick up where I left off with *Serotonin* by Michel Houellebecq. It's a novel about a chemically numbed, impotent agricultural scientist who quits his job and flees to the countryside to find happiness. He almost offs himself by jumping out of a window. He hates his job, hates his girlfriend, medicates himself out of loving or hating the unrelenting boredom. His friend blows his brains out. I'm enjoying it.

I scan one, maybe two sentences at a time before I succumb to the urge to glance up and see if Lana has snuck up to her usual spot at the north end of the pool, which gets more direct sunlight. Instead, I'm just confronted with the unendurable banality of another wasted afternoon. At this rate, it takes me five minutes to make it through each page. Sometimes I forget what I read, even though my eyes scanned all of the words, so I have to go back and read the page again. I can't help but wonder if the other residents out here notice my book or my abs or my Stone Island swim shorts or my Persol sunglasses. The answer is *probably not*, which is disappointing, but I don't bother investigating why.

I fan the pages of *Serotonin*, aimlessly guessing how many words it is and how many years it took to write. I wonder if I could do the same if I bothered to try hard enough. I wonder how many hours each day Houellebecq stared at a screen, trying to make words on the page match what was in his head. I wonder what separates people who write the story they want from the people who quit halfway through. I wonder what separates people who write important books from people who write books that are only read by the author's family before they collect dust on a shelf. I wonder if the indolent, anemic life that I've sold myself on is even compatible with making something that could be considered art.

I put the book down and Google Michel Houellebecq. Wikipedia says he was abandoned by his parents when he was a toddler, got shipped off to boarding school, and toiled away as a computer programmer while he tried to scrape together a living as a writer. He didn't make a penny from his work until he was 40 years old. I try to imagine poverty and rejection replacing the silver spoon that was shoved up my ass. Canned tuna instead of caviar. Catching the bus instead of my dad tossing me the keys to a new Mercedes for my 16th birthday. Minimum wage instead of a five-figure allowance. Maybe that version of myself would give me a story worth telling. But if I'm going to have any shot at a happy life, I have to lie to myself and say that's not true.

I didn't bother with sunscreen—I can feel my chest, face, and torso getting scorched. I lay still anyway, letting my skin char until I have a reason to leave. I'm about to doze off when my phone starts vibrating. A pit forms in my stomach when I see it's Sophia trying to FaceTime me. I can't marshal the energy for a conversation with her, so I ignore the buzzing and pick at the skin around my thumbnail until a raw pink crescent reveals itself.

I scan the pool deck one more time for Lana as my eyes drift toward the sign that says "NO LIFEGUARD ON DUTY—SWIM AT YOUR OWN RISK."

Lecture at Wally's

I'M TRYING TO GO WEST on Santa Monica, but the cars don't move even though the lights are green. They turn red green red green and I gain forty, maybe fifty feet. It's Wednesday night, and I begrudgingly agreed to meet Sophia at Wally's on North Canon at 7:00 for a "wine Wednesday rendezvous" (her words, not mine). I plan to get just drunk enough so that I'll be motivated to fuck later. The Beverly Hills location of Wally's is notoriously buzzy—the kind of place where tabloid photographers camp out for hours to snap pictures of talentless megalomaniacs with thigh gaps and C-list actors who've had the buccal fat sucked out of their faces. The thought of Sophia gawking at these semi-famous sociopaths and spewing uninvited commentary about their sex lives fills me with dread, which I fight off by reminding myself that Wally's has one of the better Bordeaux collections in LA.

While mindlessly listening to something by The Kid LAROI, I spot a CVS a block ahead on my right-hand side, which reminds me I need a Band-Aid to hide the butchered cuticles on my right index finger, but I don't have time because I'm being absolutely throttled by traffic—someone's piece-of-shit Camry stalled at the La Brea intersection.

I'm inching toward Fairfax when I see a homeless woman in her fifties trudging across the street at a glacial pace. She's wearing a tattered leopard print dress and one dirt-caked pink slipper, pushing a rusty grocery cart filled with what looks to be mostly garbage. As she ambles closer, I can see her toenails are mangled and her feet are swollen to the point where I can't distinguish her ankle bones. The skin on her legs is cracked and covered with sores that look to be crusted over with a blend of coagulated blood, pus, and dirt. She walks with a limp, dragging the slipper-less foot across the jagged pavement. It looks like she's talking to herself, something stern and hostile, but no sound is coming out, and that's when I notice she doesn't have any teeth. There are 17 seconds left on the crosswalk timer, and she's not even halfway to the sidewalk. With 12 seconds left, she tries to bend over and pick up a used cigarette but can't reach it. With five seconds left, she creeps toward a Korean couple in a Range Rover, but they look ahead and pretend she's not there. As the crosswalk timer expires and the light turns green, she's stranded in the middle of the intersection. Two Mexican guys in a Chevy pickup next to me blare their horn—she covers her ears and stares at the sky and makes the facial expression of someone who's screaming, but no sound comes out. The cars, including mine, swerve around her, and as I cross Fairfax, I turn up the volume of my music as loud as it can go.

I finally pull up to Wally's at 7:14, mumbling something polite to the valet as I realize I'm going to have to feign remorse for being late (it took me longer than expected to get my hair the way I like it). After weaving through a herd of women with starved eyes and pillowy lips, I spot Sophia trying subtly to take a picture of the Wally's sign. Normally I'm racking my brain for excuses to break up with her or at least cheat on her, but it's hard to make either of those cases right now. Her glossy brown hair is down, parted in the middle with a few barely-there waves curled through the ends. She's wearing her denim overshirt from KHAITE, wide-leg white jeans from Rag &

Bone, and a pair of Bottega Veneta stretch mules. It could be the lighting, but she looks younger, sexier. My only complaint is her red lipstick—too flamboyant, too eager.

I call Sophia's name (not in an excited way, more of a formality), and when we lock eyes, she flashes a soft, flirty smile. We kiss briefly, and I immediately wipe my lips with the back of my hand to erase any visible lipstick residue. She rests her hands on my shoulders, looks me up and down. I'm wearing my tan suede bomber jacket from Loro Piana over a linen button-down from James Perse with black trousers—also from James Perse.

"Oh my gosh babe, you look so cute I could literally *throw up*."

"I always try my best for you," I say, relieved that she's in a good mood.

"And you smell *delicious*. Is that your new Frédéric Malle cologne?"

"Tom Ford Tuscan Leather."

"Oh right. I love it! Approved."

"Should we sit?" I ask, craning my neck to scout out a decent table.

"So, I literally just put our name on the list right before you got here—she said it'll be twenty, thirty minutes max."

I shut my eyes, grit my teeth, clench my jaw, and swallow hard at the thought of standing in the packed doorway, waiting for some bimbo to give me permission to sit. It's undignified and, frankly, disgusting. I look around helplessly, accepting the reality of the situation.

"Let's get a cocktail at Il Pastaio down the street so we don't have to stand around here," I suggest, failing to mask my irritation.

"Oh that's a *cute* idea," she says, happily shrugging her shoulders.

On the way out, I involuntarily make eye contact with a middle-aged man wearing red leather cowboy boots from Enfants Richés Deprimes, stylized with silver duct tape. I almost tell him he should commit himself to a mental institution. But on the off chance he tattles to the hostess, I restrain myself so we don't lose our spot on the waitlist.

As we exit to the sidewalk, Sophia grabs hold of my hand, which is freezing cold, interlacing her fingers between mine. We walk by a group of women so blandly and predictably good-looking—layered blonde hair, radiant tans, artificially white teeth, Botoxed faces—that they fail to arouse me. Sophia squeezes my hand and speaks, bringing me back to Earth.

"Tell me about your day. What was the rose and thorn?"

"The rose and thorn?" I ask, wondering if I could convince Sophia to get a boob job.

"The high point and low point, silly goose."

I pause for a beat, looking at a Bentley Continental with a vanity plate that says "HoTNSXY."

"The low point was the traffic on Sunset. And the high point...let me think. The high point is seeing you."

She makes one of those pouty-smiley faces and gives me puppy dog eyes.

"*Stop*, really? You're such a sweetie."

"What about yours, babe?" I ask, hoping the response is something that won't warrant too much effort to comprehend. "Rose and thorn."

"Okay, so, my high point was that I absolutely *crushed* my heated Pilates class this morning and didn't even have to take any breaks. And Sydney—you know, the instructor who's dating the chef who we think might be gay—she said my deep core strength is some of the best she's ever seen. We focused on glutes today and I can already tell I'm going to be sore, but in, like, a good way."

"And the low point?"

"Well," she says tentatively. "Coco had a little...*accident* on the rug while I was at work."

"I thought Coco was done having accidents."

"It's just...she gets separation anxiety while I'm away."

"That's unfortunate."

"*Stop.*" She playfully smacks my shoulder. "Coco's my good baby girl. She just misses her momma."

We walk in silence until we get to the bar at Il Pastaio, where a podgy old man with flushed cheeks and dyed hair is sitting with a hollow-eyed redhead half his age. Her tits are so big they're practically resting in her lap. They're slouched over martini glasses, murmuring something about a carjacking on La Cienega, and it's obvious that the man has a tick or maybe some kind of disorder, but I can't place it. A bartender in a crisp white Oxford shirt sets down two coasters, and before he has a chance to greet us, I immediately order a Negroni (Monkey 47 gin). Sophia orders an espresso martini (Grey Goose).

"So," Sophia clasps her hands together. "I want to know more about your book. I can't believe I'm dating an *author.*"

This question shifts my mental state from boredom to panic. I reach for my drink but realize there's only a glass of lukewarm tap water.

"What do you want to know?" I ask, stalling.

"Well, for starters I'd like to know what it's *about*."

I force a playful chuckle, fingering the damp napkin as the gears of my mind sputter.

"The main character, he's a teenager, and he's desperate to get famous—infamous—on the internet."

"And...what about him?" She asks this playfully, but it registers as confrontational.

"And he's willing to commit horrific, unspeakable acts to make that happen."

There's a painfully long pause as "Summer Wind" by Frank Sinatra plays in the background.

"That sounds...not very nice. What made you want to write something dark like that?"

I consider telling her the truth: That I'm desperate to shed my reputation as a sickeningly spoiled nepo baby who can't accomplish anything on his own. That I need to manipulate people into giving me the validation I've denied myself. That I have a compulsive need to be seen as exceptional and superior. But I'm unable and unwilling to access that level of vulnerability so I formulate an alternate response—the good reason, not the real reason.

"I'm fascinated by the intersection of...psychology and media. I think we're in a cultural moment right now, and I want to capture the essence of it, reflect it back to society in a way that makes people reevaluate where we're headed. I mean, the other day, I read a story about a kid who almost died while trying to eat 10,000 calories' worth of Intense Nacho Takis and nobody seemed to think that was a problem."

"Is there...a plot? Maybe this kid gets hacked, or blackmailed—no wait, *both*. He gets hacked and blackmailed and the bad guys give him one week to send them a million dollars or else they kill him. How about *that*?"

She watches me, wide-eyed, waiting for approval.

"No, I don't think so," I say, watching the bartender stir my Negroni mechanically.

"Isn't it kind of a boring story, then?"

I sigh, realizing no degree of articulation will convince Sophia that my idea has merit.

"The greatest books ever written sound boring if you just describe the plot: A millionaire on Long Island wants to shack up with his former lover. A boat captain wants to get revenge against a whale. A family migrates from Oklahoma to California during the Dust Bowl. The only thing that actually matters is if the writer makes you feel something. A man like Henry Miller could write about doing the fucking dishes and have you on the edge of your seat."

"Or a *woman*—you know they can write too."

"Right," I say, "That too."

Our drinks mercifully arrive, and I take a large swig of my Negroni. It has a touch too much Campari, but I would've settled for Bud Light at this point. It burns my chest as it goes down, and it feels good. Feels right. Sophia takes a sip of her espresso martini, leaving a perfectly symmetrical red lipstick stain on the rim of the glass.

"Ooof, that's *strong*. Want a sip?"

"I'm good."

She fidgets in her barstool. Looks for the next sentence in the creamy beige foam of her drink.

"Are you okay? I mean, I know you're super busy at work, and now you're writing this book. But something seems, I don't know, *off*?"

If I had any balls, I'd put an end to this right now. I'd describe to her, in graphic detail, the times I cheated on her with Lana and the travel influencer and the Brazilian medical student and the waitress from Horses. I'd tell her our relationship feels like a prison sentence. I'd tell her I don't give a shit about the house in Santa Barbara she'll eventually inherit or how compatible we are on an astrological basis or the half marathon that she deludes herself into thinking is a real accomplishment. I'd tell her it's hilarious that she thinks I need any of this. I'd tell her all of that and maybe even more and I'd hand the bartender a crisp hundred-dollar bill and walk out the door and delete her number and erase every half-hearted fuck session out of my memory. But I'm too much of a coward to complicate the narrative, so I drown my pretend monologue with another huge swig of my Negroni and tell the lie I've told a thousand times before.

"I'm just feeling...burnt out, that's all—overwhelmed. You know how I get. If something was wrong between us, I'd tell you."

She rotates her martini glass slowly on the bar top, studying the three espresso beans with great interest.

"You promise?" she asks sheepishly.

"One hundred percent," I assure her.

"I guess sometimes I just get a little...*nervous* about where we stand. I feel like the longer we're together, the more mysterious you are to me."

How much longer can this go on? I ask myself. *How is this possible?*

"You know how I get sometimes," I say, immediately realizing I said the exact same thing a few seconds ago. "I get lost in my own head, and now I'm lost in my book. Things will work out. *We'll* work out. You know how special you are to me. You're amazing. You're beautiful. You're talented."

I want to rip a cuticle off my finger, but Sophia places her hand on top of mine and gives me a soft kiss on the cheek. I feel nothing.

"That's all I needed to hear."

Her phone lights up and buzzes—a text from Wally's telling us our table is ready. I toss back the rest of my Negroni and walk toward the exit, feeling the guy with dyed hair staring at me. I feel a light buzz in my head, but it's not enough, not nearly enough, to make me feel how I want.

The hostess at Wally's seats us at a high-top, which we have to share with six other people. The couple next to us looks to be in their late thirties, maybe early forties. I haven't had a good look at the man because he's right next to me, but the woman has a face that's been horribly maimed by what must have been at least a dozen plastic surgeries and I can't stop gawking. Her eyelids are pinned upward, the tissue around her cheekbones looks like it was attacked by bees, her eyebrows are stuck in permanent, exaggerated arches, and I notice her face doesn't move when she laughs, speaks, or eats.

Our waiter arrives impressively quick with menus. I'm desperate for alcohol, so I ask him to send the sommelier over. The plastic woman across from me keeps asserting to the man that she's an extroverted introvert.

"What's new at work, babe?" Sophia asks. "Last time you told me there was some drama about a big toothpaste campaign coming up."

"Yeah, toothpaste. I think I finally got that under control. The people at KBM love to overcomplicate what we do, like it's a math problem or something."

"And what is it really?"

"It's just telling people what they want to believe."

"What do they want to believe?"

I scan the room, a menagerie of high-functioning narcissists.

"They want to believe there's a version of themselves worth becoming."

The sommelier, who introduces himself as Paul, arrives and asks what we're in the mood for. I tell him we want a Bordeaux, something rich and full-bodied with a streak of acidity. Paul's eyes light up.

"I have something *perfect* for you two: a 2018 Château Pape Clement. It comes from the oldest estate in Bordeaux—the soil composition allows for a healthy dose of Merlot, which brings a decadent, velvety character to the wine. This bottle in particular comes from 66% Cabernet Sauvignon, 30% Merlot, and the rest Cabernet Franc brought up in 60% new French oak. It's a gorgeous wine that actually performs even better from bottle than barrel, which is always a good sign. It's deep garnet-purple with stunning crème de cassis and blackberry fruits, as well as kaleidoscope-like notes of graphite, scorched earth, smoke, violets, and spring flowers. You get this full-bodied richness, but it stays light on its feet. The Cabernet Sauvignon really sings at this point, and there's almost a Médoc-like regalness to it."

"That'll work," I murmur, avoiding eye contact with an effete man at the bar who keeps flashing a toothy smile in my direction.

"Excellent."

Sophia cuts in.

"And could you please send our waiter over when you get a chance? We want to order a little snack or two."

"Of course, ma'am."

Paul wanders off and I hope it doesn't take long to get our wine, because the buzz from my Negroni is already tapering off. To distract myself, I muster up the enthusiasm to ask Sophia a question about her job.

"How's the Spanish Colonial Revival project going? The one in Beverly Hills."

"You mean the one in Bel-Air?"

"Yeah, that one."

"Well, the bones of the house are strong—original Spanish tilework, exposed wood-beamed ceilings. But the old owners left the interior feeling disjointed. It doesn't need a total overhaul, just some attention to the details that were already there." Sophia is like a wind-up doll, you can tee up the most basic question and she'll just go until someone stops her. She continues. "While we were peeling back the layers, we kept asking ourselves, 'Will this be relevant in five years? Ten years? Fifteen years? The owners wanted the home to feel authentic to its Spanish Colonial style, but still fresh and current. People don't understand that it usually takes more work to *restore* than it does to build something *new*."

As I nod along, I see Paul out of the corner of my eye.

"Obviously," she continues, "we'll have to make some compromises between contemporary luxury and functionality.

Like in the kitchen, we'll keep the center island but reconfigure the space to allow for a more generous flow and…"

"I'm sorry to interrupt," says Paul. "Your 2018 Château Pape Clement."

I give Paul an impatient nod. As he uncorks the bottle Sophia says something about gold Calcutta marble and all I can think about is how badly I want to escape into solitude. Paul pours an ounce of wine into my glass. I swirl and sniff and suck on it, as if pulling it through a straw, which aerates the wine and circulates it throughout your mouth (I learned this with my parents during a trip to Provence when I was 17). The wine tastes like ripe berries at first, followed by cardamom and cacao.

"We love it," I tell Paul.

"Excellent," he says, filling our glasses. "Enjoy, you two."

"So *anyway*," Sophia says. "Our ultimate goal is a home that's equal parts refined and casual, which I think we can achieve by combining simple furniture silhouettes layered with vintage textiles."

"It sounds like you're really coming into your own at the firm, babe."

"I just wish *Edgar* felt that way. Sometimes I just feel so *invalidated* around him and the other partners. Plus, I was supposed to get a raise like two months ago and they keep delaying my performance review."

Edgar is her boss—rich but not wealthy, probably in the closet, definitely addicted to cocaine and possibly Xanax too.

"He'll come around," I tell her.

I take a large sip of the 2018 Château Pape Clement and I'm immediately tempted to slug the entire glass. I'm purposely avoiding my glass of water so I can feel the alcohol faster. The couple next to us is getting up to leave and the plastic woman trips, nearly falling out of her chair and her face still doesn't move. Our waiter arrives and Sophia orders truffle fries with grated parmesan.

"Mmm, what do you think of the wine, babe?"

"It drinks well, but I wouldn't say it blows me away."

I surprise myself by how quickly the bottle empties as the night progresses. Sophia only has one glass and I have four. Each sip makes me hungrier, and even though I'm terrified of losing the abs that I've worked tirelessly to sculpt, I can't resist the salty, savory, fatty temptation in front of me. So I indulge. With my inhibitions rapidly unwinding, I come extremely close to ordering a second bottle of 2018 Château Pape Clement, but it's a weeknight so I rein myself in and order a dirty gin martini (Hendricks) with three blue cheese olives. This should be enough to tide me over for the night. It arrives quickly and I take a large swig, reducing my world to a hazy blur while pretending to listen as Sophia tells me about an actress at the bar who has a minor role in an upcoming Hulu drama. I stare into Sophia's eyes, going in and out of focus. She thinks I'm being flirty, but really I'm wondering how I let myself get to this point and whether I'll ever have the balls to change the narrative.

"What a fun Wine Wednesday date night," she says, taking a bite out of a truffle fry, chewing it seductively before licking her lips. "Love this for us. I just need to make sure we get back to my place soon so I can let Coco out."

By now the alcohol has melted away whatever filter I maintained throughout the night. My urge to say something hurtful is bubbling up from somewhere deep inside me, and by the time I realize this, it's too late to stop myself.

"Speaking of Coco," I say, leaning back.

"What about my sweet baby girl?"

"Don't take this the wrong way, but if you have a dog and you're trying to get ahead in an industry as cutthroat as yours, you're not really serious about succeeding."

I punctuate this sentence with a silence that gives it depth and dimension. She glares at me as I pop a blue cheese olive into my mouth.

"I know you have big goals and aspirations and dreams," I say, chewing ravenously. "But if you're actually serious about getting on Edgar's level, if you really want to run shit, it's just not going to happen if you have a dog."

Her face is frozen still, except for her lower lip quivering.

"If you want to light the world on fire, if you want to have *Architectural Digest* drooling over your work, but you've decided it's more important to scoop kibble and pick up shit and sweep fur balls and leave events early to make it home before your couch gets pissed on, you're sabotaging your chance at real success."

She stares.

"Which is fine," I say before knocking back the rest of my martini. "But just admit that to yourself. I know a lot of people—nice people, good people—who say they want to make a bunch of money or start a business or whatever. But they go, 'I have a dog.' And I can't help but think how fucking insane that is."

The look on Sophia's face is unlike anything I've seen before, some horrible combination of sadness and disgust.

"What the fuck is wrong with you?" she finally asks.

"It's just the truth. It's the reality. You weigh yourself down. I know you love that dog. But let's be very honest: She's not helping you get anywhere in life. It's just that...time is so valuable. And that's what so many people don't understand."

"You're drunk," she says, as if that's a legitimate excuse for my outburst. I've hurt her deeply, but I don't care because it felt good.

"I just want the best for you," I sigh.

"I think *I* can figure out what's best for me. Talk to me when you figure out how to handle alcohol like an adult."

She grabs her Louis Vuitton pochette and storms away from the table, bumping into a clearly-drunk Persian guy in an ill-fitting Balmain t-shirt, and a wave of relief washes over me. The waiter, who probably watched this unfold from some unseen vantage point, drops the check in front of me, which is, to my surprise, only $240. I'm in a generous mood, so I tip $60 to make it an even $300. I stumble into the bathroom where I take a long piss, swaying slightly in front of the urinal before leaving the restaurant and retrieving my car from the valet who I don't tip because I'm out of cash. As I'm speeding down Santa Monica, wondering if I'll make it home without getting a DUI or causing some sort of grim accident, I see the homeless woman from earlier. She's still staring at the sky and screaming, but no sound is coming out.

When I get home, I sprawl on my couch and masturbate to a video in which a petite blonde real estate agent hosts a potential buyer for a house tour. The price is a steep, even though it's been on the market for six months, so the

Dominic Vaiana

agent persuades him to pay the asking price by blowing him in the kitchen (which is decorated horrifically). This is followed by intercourse on the sofa, in the shower, and finally in the master bedroom. I ejaculate weakly, barely feeling anything, take a scalding hot shower, then lay in bed watching videos of alleged UFOs caught on Ring doorbell cameras in the suburbs of Las Vegas until I fall asleep.

Chapter One

I WAKE UP AT 5:48 from a shallow, dreamless sleep on Sunday morning, immediately confronted by the vast emptiness of the upcoming day—no appointments, no dinner reservations, no aimless trips to the Brentwood farmer's market with Sophia. Things between us have been rocky since our spat at Wally's last Wednesday, even though I reluctantly admitted, over text, that my rant about prioritizing her dog over her career was "probably a little aggressive."

After a failed attempt to lull myself back to sleep, I grab my phone and scroll mechanically through Instagram—a tour of a newly-listed property in Benedict Canyon, a D-list actress I matched with on Raya last year sipping wine at the cheapest five-star hotel in Milan, an ad for a red light helmet to stimulate hair growth—while half-thinking of ways to kill the next fifteen hours until I can drink myself to sleep. I could ask my hairstylist to squeeze me in for a touch-up around the sideburns, which I don't really need; drive out to the John Varvatos store at Malibu Country Mart to buy the lamb leather trench coat I've had my eye on (it's out of stock in my size at their West Hollywood and Century City stores); go to Cecconi's for a solo brunch on the patio; get the Porsche detailed. The reality is that all of these activities require a level of effort that I'm not willing to exert on a Sunday, and I'll end up idling at the pool until I find a woman hot enough to approach. But I'm gutted when I check my weather app and see the forecast is mostly cloudy and 67 degrees with a UV index of 2—the only cloudy day for the next week.

Effectively out of viable options, I masturbate to a video of two playful Korean women having a threesome with an unwitting customer at a massage parlor, take a 20-minute shower, order a Coconut Cloud smoothie from Erewhon via Postmates ($34 with delivery fees, tax, and tip), and try to finish a chapter of *Serotonin* on the couch before finally coming to grips with the fact that I haven't worked on my book in four days. I halfheartedly walk to my desk, and as I force myself to double-click the document that I titled "Chapter 1," my palms actually start to sweat—some terrible blend of anxiety and shame bubbling up inside my chest.

I brace myself before checking the word count: 96.

I silently read the lone paragraph I cobbled together the other day: a teenage boy in geometry class, watching a prank video where a guy fake-sneezes on people in a grocery store using a water bottle. The teacher kicks him and his friend out. It's not dark. It's not provocative. It's not even weird. It's just boring—the literary equivalent of elevator music. I scan those lines over and over, as if repetition might alchemize it into something that sucks less. But then I realize with an acid awareness that I can't share this with anyone, especially a literary agent or editor.

I stare at the blinking cursor and wonder how long it will take to finish my novel at this glacial pace. I've read plenty of short books that won awards and changed the world and earned the authors a lot of respect, so I start Googling. *The Stranger* by Albert Camus page count: 123 pages. *Ask the Dust* by John Fante page count: 165 pages. *The Trial* by Kafka page count: 166 pages (he technically didn't finish it because he starved to death—a severe case of laryngeal tuberculosis made it too painful for him to eat).

My research gives me some reassurance that I won't have to spend years slaving away at my manuscript. I arbitrarily decide that 152 pages is a respectable length, especially since modern readers can barely watch a TikTok without losing focus. I Google "how many words is 152 pages?" and I see that it's about 42,000 words, assuming each formatted page of the book fits about 275 words. I tell myself I can write 500 words per day if I really try. I open the calculator app on my MacBook, divide 42,000 by 500, and find the magic number: 84. I can have a completed first draft of a novel in 84 days, just before Christmas.

I try to stare at the blinking cursor, but my eyes inadvertently drift away from the page, out past the perfectly manicured Bermuda grass of The Los Angeles Country Club toward the towers in Westwood and Century City. I think of some podcast where a pop psychologist said you're supposed to start typing even if the sentences are shitty, even if it reads like a cry for help, just to build momentum.

But I don't want to write something shitty. I want to write something that will impress and shock and command attention and I want it to happen instantaneously. I want the letters and words and sentences and paragraphs and pages to flow effortlessly through my fingertips and I want those pages to mirror exactly what's in my head, with little to no editing required. I want to absolve myself from any struggle or pain along this journey, and even though I know that both are necessary to make anything meaningful, I'm going to pretend it's not true. I stare out of my sterile glass box and wait for those words and ideas to arrive in my head, but they don't come. I have nothing to show for my time, but I'm mentally drained and I'm craving stimulation, so I start Googling around for coffee shops that look aesthetic enough to write at.

I pull the Porsche onto North San Vicente, sporting my limited edition Persol 714SM sunglasses even though it's mostly cloudy, and turn on Today's Hits. The first song is about smoking weed and fucking your ex-girlfriend in a car outside of a club. Coming down the opposite side of the street is the red TMZ Celebrity Tour bus. Every day, it departs from the Hard Rock Cafe in Hollywood. For $59, you can ride around for two hours and have some loser show you where celebrities have allegedly been spotted eating, drinking, shopping, and socializing. TMZ tells the tourists they could see stars such as Mariah Carey, Justin Bieber, Rihanna, and Dwayne "The Rock" Johnson, although they can't legally make any guarantees because people have sued them for false advertising. All 25 seats inside the bus have USB charging ports to ensure the tourists have plenty of battery power in case they want to take videos or snap photos of celebrities in the wild. I pass directly by the bus and look at the passengers through my Persols. Most of them are obese and sunburnt with facial expressions that look to be a combination of hopefulness and embarrassment. A few of them just stare at their phones.

I park outside of a new French café on Melrose called L'essence, which *Los Angeles Magazine* called "iconic" last week. The all-day lobby café and lounge fuses a Bauhaus influence with a minimalist aesthetic: taupe concrete floors, exposed white-glazed brick walls, original art by Hans Dubuffer, George Hartrung, and Jean Condo.

The noon rush is a herd of detestable pick-me people. A girl in an Aviator Nation sweatsuit chases her flea-infested mongrel that barks incessantly, drowning out "Paperbacks" by Arlo Parks, which is playing on a turntable. A man with a mustache, frosted tips, and overalls diligently arranges his cortado and book in the natural light so he can snap a photo with his Polaroid. I do a double-take and notice it's a copy of *Feral Symphony*: "the book America deserves."

The crowd is frantic but directionless. They smile and chatter and nod and take little sips from ceramic mugs and nibble croissants that flake onto the small marble tables, never bothering to clean up after themselves. These people look to be my age, but I don't feel any sense of connection to them. I can't explain why, but I think it's because they're brimming with naive optimism. And why shouldn't they be? It's easy to be happy if you don't think, if you don't demand anything of yourself. You can just be an empty vessel that fills up with whatever the world shoves down your throat: run clubs, pickleball, ketamine, red light facials, psychedelic mushrooms, pretending to be sober, trying to live forever, astrocartography, shamanic breathwork, Joshua Tree, manifestation, cryptocurrency, Coachella, natural wine, tantric sex, tarot cards, dry fasting—all stuff you can do while waiting to die.

I walk up to the live-edge wood counter, standing behind a couple radiating the performative indifference of people desperate for attention. The guy, sporting a precisely tousled mullet, wears baggy trousers, a pair of chunky Derby shoes, and a Carhartt Detroit jacket layered over a white tank top. His girlfriend leans against his shoulder, hair held back by oversized tortoiseshell sunglasses, wearing a cropped tee and white linen pants. They murmur to each other in tones too low to decipher (I pick up something about a cabin in

Topanga), but the occasional burst of laughter, hollow and rehearsed, pierces the air.

After the happy couple finally fucks off, I order a single-origin pour-over: Ethiopia, Yabitu Koba Region, altitude 2,100 mean sea level. The menu says it has tasting notes of apricot, kumquat, and butterscotch. With tax and tip, it's $9.

I claim an empty table in the back corner, where I set my black Paul Smith embossed leather backpack. The douchebag next to me has skin the color of printer paper, and he's emaciated to the point where it looks like he might have some type of cancer or autoimmune disease. His distressed leather jacket smells like it just came out of a Goodwill donation bin, and his green Carhartt beanie only covers the top fourth of his shaved head. His facial structure resembles that of a bird's. The font on his screen is Courier—probably a screenplay or pilot doomed to fail. For a second, I hate myself because we're both the same hateable species: space-hogging, oxygen-sucking Wi-Fi thieves typing words on a screen that will likely amount to nothing. But then I remind myself that I have a higher net worth, better home amenities, a faster car, and a more optimal muscle-to-bodyfat ratio. I can't prove any of this, but in order to move forward with the rest of my day, I have to believe it.

"Pour over for Nathan," the barista barks in a tone that makes it clear she loathes her job, but loathes serving someone like me even more.

I retrieve my small porcelain cup on a tin platter and bring it back to my table, but immediately realize I need the Wi-Fi password to access my Google Drive. I refuse to ask the emaciated screenwriter for the password, so I walk back up to the counter and ask the cranky barista. I feel like a loser and a fraud because Don DeLillo didn't need a Wi-Fi password or a $9 cup of coffee to write *White Noise*. The barista scoffs and juts her chin toward a tiny sign on the wall that displays the password: "GoodVibes90210."

I return to my laptop (15-inch MacBook Air with Liquid Retina display and an M2 chip), connect to the Wi-Fi, and open my document titled "Chapter 1" for the second time today. I stare at the blinking cursor. The emaciated screenwriter is typing at a quick pace. He seems calm, focused, almost Zen-like. He uncrosses, recrosses, and uncrosses his legs. I think about dumping my $9 coffee on his laptop and storming off, but I recalibrate and remind myself that I need to write 500 words every day so I can have a completed manuscript before Christmas. I place my fingers on the keyboard and notice a piece of dry, dead skin on the inside of my left thumbnail. I pry it loose, unleashing a thin, precise stream of blood along my nail bed. I smear it on my black Reiss jeans, but it pools up again quickly.

The screenwriter is typing at a feverish pace, taunting me. I take a large gulp of my coffee, which scalds the roof of my mouth, making it impossible to taste the notes of apricot, kumquat, and butterscotch. I check my phone—Sophia texted me about going to watch the sunset in Temescal Canyon Park. I turn the phone on Do Not Disturb. I look back at my laptop and stare at the blinking cursor. It says you're soft and lazy and a fucking fraud. I take three large gulps from my mug, and it's empty. The couple next to me is discussing intergenerational trauma over a piece of $14 pistachio toast.

I slam my MacBook shut and tell myself I'll write 1,000 words tomorrow to make up for writing zero words today.

My Dad's Birthday Party

I CAN'T HANG OUT with my family sober, so I'm taking pulls of Hendrick's out of a flask at a stoplight on San Vicente, trying to avoid eye contact with a one-armed flower vendor. Today is my dad's 61st birthday, so my parents are hosting the local relatives at their house for dinner. His gift is on the passenger seat of the Porsche: a bottle of 2005 Domaine Philippe Leclerc Les Cazetiers and a pair of Brunello Cucinelli suede loafers, size twelve.

The spotlight will be on my dad tonight, but I'm bracing myself for at least three hours of recycled banter about what's going on in my relatives' lives—how it might rain in Barbados and ruin their annual vacation, the nonstop home renovations to outdo each other, their kids' meaningless academic achievements. I've trained myself to maintain a baseline level of courtesy by not getting completely fucked up at family parties. But enduring the night with an ABV of zero is out of the question, so I polish off the rest of my Hendrick's as I turn left on red.

Sophia would normally tag along to something like this, but she's been in Santa Barbara all weekend for her sister's 30th birthday. The timing is ideal, since we got into an argument over FaceTime yesterday about why I removed my tag from a picture she posted of us on Instagram. Sophia doesn't know how to control her emotions, and my family would sniff out the tension as soon as we walked in the door.

Unfortunately, her absence won't absolve me from someone half-drunk and faux-sincere asking me "how things are going" with Sophia—a poorly concealed attempt to gauge whether they should expect an engagement sometime soon. So I rehearse all of my stock phrases, letting the gin work its magic:

My favorite part about Sophia is that she gets me out of my shell and brings out the best version of myself.

Sophia and I make a great couple because we push each other to excel socially and professionally, but never at the expense of our individual happiness.

Sophia and I want to travel abroad more next year—Osaka is at the top of our list.

It's all bullshit, of course. But honesty isn't an acceptable language with this crowd. It's more important that I spoon-feed my relatives the innocuous platitudes they crave so I don't disrupt the anesthetizing sameness, the uncomplicated narrative, that everyone works tirelessly to maintain.

I turn onto Sunset, which curves and dips and winds. My vision briefly stutters as the Riviera Country Club comes into view. My dad desperately wants me to follow in his footsteps and join, but I hate the sport and hate the people who play it even more. The maddeningly slow pace that caters to the geriatric and the indolent, the vapid chit-chat about approaches and fades and punches, the smugness of deadbeat fathers and absent husbands who devote more than half of their waking hours to this pathetic escape from reality—all of it has infuriated me since the time I picked up a TaylorMade driver for the first time in the fifth grade. Despite voicing these complaints, my dad still clings to the belief that I'll "come around to the beauty of the game." He bought me a $7,500 set of clubs for my 21st birthday, which is currently sitting in a storage unit in Ladera Heights.

As the setting sun glints through my windshield, I'm struck with childhood memories of my parents driving us up this road on the way back from dinner or tennis lessons or some art exhibition. They'd rattle on about the lyrical passagework of a cello concerto or the astonishing depth of flavor in a cassoulet. I wanted to join those conversations, but I kept my mouth shut because I was terrified of saying something dumb or incorrect and disappointing them. Instead, I'd just stare at the canyons outside the tinted window of my dad's Jaguar XJ. I'd make up stories in my head about aliens and monsters. Count backwards from one million. Imagine getting on a plane and moving far away, maybe someplace where it snowed.

My childhood, I'm frequently reminded, was idyllic: safe, spoiled, pain-free. I could have acted out if I wanted to, could have taken up arms against the numbing opulence. I could have dyed my hair green, sold ecstasy, desecrated my body with tattoos, screamed into a microphone at a warehouse in downtown LA, whatever. I knew a few kids who revolted, at least through their college years. But I could never summon the energy to really go off the rails. I craved attention, but I was too scared to ask for it. So I behaved and did all the right things and followed all the rules. I compensated by rebelling with my thoughts, fantasizing about how I might build a life that was raw and real and undeniably my own, a life that wasn't preordained by my last name. I guess I was happy, but happy in the expectation that something else would happen—some wonderful, unnamed thing I was destined for, but couldn't define.

Thinking about my childhood makes my chest constrict and my eye twitch, so I turn up the volume on Today's Hits—it's a song about a hot girl popping her pussy and shaking her ass and dropping it to the floor. As I'm chewing a handful of Altoids, failing to mask my gin-soaked breath, I pull the Porsche up to my parents' driveway toward their home, an all-white mid-century build—five beds, seven baths, 5,500 square feet, surrounded by tall hedges and a wooden gate. Five cars glisten in the driveway (all of which were obviously detailed this afternoon to show off), including my uncle Brad's 1962 Mercedes-Benz 190SL.

I check the clock on my dashboard: 5:52—I took the long way to arrive intentionally late so I could avoid solo time with my parents. As I walk up the floating concrete steps to the oversized front door, I imagine I should feel some type of nostalgia. There should be a montage of pleasant memories playing in my head: mom and dad pushing me on a swing set; blowing out candles at birthday parties; baking cookies with my mom, fingers and face covered with icing. But these aren't the memories that come to mind. Instead, there's just this oceanic sense of dread and raging helplessness that manifests itself as a churning in my stomach, cold fingers, and a tight jaw.

Before I have a chance to ring the doorbell, the door swings open and I'm greeted by my mom, who gives me a hesitant hug and a cold peck on the cheek. I tell her it's nice to see her. She says I look tired. My dad steps out from behind her. Even though he's an inch and a half shorter than I am, it feels like I'm looking up at his pastel blue eyes, which are somehow striking but vacant. He tells me I need a haircut. I wish him a happy birthday, and he shakes my hand clinically before thanking me, glancing skeptically at the gifts I didn't bother wrapping.

They walk me into the living room like a show pony, where my aunts, uncles, and cousins are sipping champagne and nibbling on what appears to be some kind of shrimp hors d'oeuvre. L-O-V-E by Nat King Cole trickles out of the Sonos sound system. Everyone flashes tight, controlled smiles in unison—more reflex than an expression of joy. The first to greet me is my dad's youngest brother, Brad, a mergers and acquisitions attorney who splits his time between Malibu and New York. He has a chiseled jaw, skin flushed red from testosterone replacement therapy, and a forehead so shiny I can see my reflection in it.

"What's the word, player?" he says, revealing a mouthful of pristine white veneers, which were installed by the same cosmetic dentist responsible for the smiles of Kris Jenner and Charlie Sheen.

"You know, just trying to make it happen," I sigh.

"From what your dad tells me, it sounds like you're doing more than just making it happen. I still can't get over that commercial you did for Hellmann's Mayonnaise a few months ago—the one where Jon Hamm and Brie Larson are stuck in the fridge and Pete Davidson threatens to eat them. Chloe and I thought it was pure gold."

Chloe is Brad's third wife—a 32-year-old Barbie doll with a self-diagnosed mood disorder that she treats with lorazepam. Last Christmas, her spray tan got all over my parents' white Poltrona Frau sofa, so Brad had to pay $2,500 to get it cleaned.

"*Soooo good*, Nate. Did they give you any free mayonnaise after that?" she asks, cackling to herself.

"Unfortunately not," I say, looking around for a drink to grab. "But the check cleared."

"That's all that matters, player," says Brad. "How 'bout we get Ogilvy Junior over here a glass of champagne to celebrate his old man?"

We walk into the kitchen, which my parents recently finished renovating. My dad is more eager to lecture us about the finishes than he is to see me: lozenge-shaped skylights, twin kitchen islands topped in emerald quartzite, stools by Studio Van den Akker, custom brass hardware by Pashupatina, sink fittings by Waterworks, and floors by Hermosa Terrazzo. Brad pours me and my dad a glass of Krug Grande Cuvée 170ème Édition Brut. We cheer each other, take a sip, and I immediately want another because I know the buzz from my road gin won't last much longer. We join the rest of the family in the living room, where I'm immediately cornered by my aunt Catherine. She's running her mouth about a new novel she bought, and as soon as I hear the words "subway rat" my eyes glaze over. The book America deserves.

"*Feral Symphony* is the name of it," she says. "And the author, oh, I forget his name, they're saying he's the millennials' Vonnegut."

"Does it live up to the hype?" I ask.

"Well, I haven't read it quite yet," she admits. "But I had to order a copy after I read his profile in the *Times*—I mean, how could you not fall in love with this guy?"

I excuse myself to take a piss, but instead I make a detour to the kitchen where I slug a glass and a half of 2016 Louis Jadot Clos Saint-Jacques Pinot Noir before anybody has a chance to catch me. I feel the wine blot out the looming trepidations, slowly transforming me into a more agreeable, more placid Nathan. As I stagger back through the hallway to the living room, my gaze drifts toward a shelf lined with family photographs. My parents must have added this display as part of the renovation, because I can't remember seeing it before. A worried little boy clutching a baseball bat in the driveway. A family of three, deep tans and forced smiles, squinting in the sunlight on the Manhattan Beach pier. A father and his son at a high school graduation ceremony, standing with an awkward space between them. I feel a shiver and notice that I'm gripping my wine glass so hard that the flesh under my fingernails is white.

Over the next hour, I drift from conversation to conversation, which I participate in, or at least imagine I do. My aunt Julia's dog walker (a 38-year-old failed actor) recently had abdominal etching surgery, where unwanted fat around his torso was strategically liposuctioned from his body in an attempt to contour the abdominal muscles and create a six-pack overnight. She says it looks scary. My uncle Lawrence tells everyone, for the second time, that he's investing $1.5 million in a San Francisco-based startup that makes cell-cultivated meat. It requires a fermentation process involving bioreactors, and that's where the money is—not in the meat itself, but in the bioreactors. My three-year-old cousin is making good marks at the Center for Early Education, a preschool in West Hollywood that costs $23,000 per year. Her favorite subject is French. One of Brad's partners at the law firm got belligerently drunk after a fundraiser for colon cancer and crashed his Range Rover into a light pole at 88 miles per hour. He walked away virtually unscathed, but his wife, who was in the passenger seat, suffered a lacerated abdomen and recently learned that the injury has rendered her infertile. For brief moments I disassociate and think about Lana's tits or the lobster sauce cavatelli I want to try at Pasta | Bar or oblique exercises or the video I was watching earlier about a guy who filled his entire swimming pool with Skittles.

The sun finally sets, and my mom announces that dinner is ready in the formal dining room. She made my dad's favorite: beef bourguignon garnished with pearl onions, mushrooms, and bacon. I have a solid buzz that makes me feel somewhere between tolerant and affable. I remember sitting in this dining room as a small child, and I would rarely speak because I was afraid I might say something dumb or incorrect and disappoint my parents. Instead of replaying those memories for the second time today, I take a large gulp of my 2010 Comte Armand Clos des Epeneaux Monopole.

My cousin Louis, who graduated from Cornell last spring, blabs about the key role he's playing in the acquisition of a mattress company at the private equity firm he works for. Louis is taller and has a slightly darker tan than mine, although he's not as lean and his hair is already beginning to thin at the crown of his head. I tune out most of what he's saying, but pick up terms like "due diligence," "value creation," and "carried interest." I nod and chew the beef, which seems blander than the last time I had it.

Louis shouts across the table, gesturing at me with his fork.

"Nate, you've had your poker face on all night. Everyone's bored with my mattress stories. Give us a glimpse into the advertising biz. What are they paying you guys to shill these days?"

I wash down my beef with the 2010 Comte, deciding if I want to play along with Louis or antagonize him.

"Toothpaste, this week. We should get the Cheez-It account next month if we play our cards right."

"Toothpaste and Cheez-Its—what more does America need?"

Everyone laughs, my father the loudest.

"I feel like I've asked you this a million times, but what exactly do you do over there?" he asks.

"I'm the Executive Creative Director," I say distantly.

"So, what? Do you write taglines and all that?"

"Sometimes," I say, pushing a mushroom around with my fork. "The copywriters usually handle it."

"And you have to convince the clients to sign off on your big ideas?"

"That's what account managers are for."

"So you just sit around and...*make stuff up*?"

"Sure."

Louis swirls his wine and raises his eyebrows.

"Quite the job description for an executive."

My uncle Brad clears his throat.

"Say what you want about Nate, but he climbed the ranks pretty quickly over there at—at uh..."

"KBM," my mother reminds him.

"That's right. And you did it all before you turned 30. Plus, you're a voracious reader from what your dad tells me. Will, Janice—you two did a hell of a job with this kid. This *rockstar*."

My mom and dad nod as we lapse into an embarrassing silence. At first I don't want to vocalize what I'm thinking, but

I feel an immediate and intense urge to command everyone's approval.

"I've actually been spending more time writing than reading," I say, feeling my pulse rise and my chest constrict.

"Writing?" Brad asks, baffled. "Writing what, checks?"

Cackles break out. The desperation escalates.

"A book," I say coolly, and then: "A novel."

Everyone raises their eyes simultaneously. An ominous silence washes over the dining room as I glance around, desperate for a shred of validation. My mom is the first one to speak.

"Well, this is such *exciting* news," she says, trying to reassure me with an upward inflection. "How long has that been in the works, Nate?"

I shrug.

"A few weeks, maybe a month."

I don't have to look at my dad to know he's confused and concerned.

"Well, are you going to tell us what your book is about?" my aunt Catherine asks.

I try to piece together something coherent on the fly, but all I can think about is my dad's glare.

"It's about this kid, a teenager, who's trying to go viral with these videos he makes," I stammer, on the verge of a breakdown. "And he's willing to commit horrific, unspeakable acts to make that happen."

Mostly everyone nods, but they seem either uninterested or unimpressed. Brad utters the lone "mmm," which echoes inside the dining room walls. I run my middle finger along the nail bed of my thumb until I find a piece of dead skin that I can tear away to distract myself from the shame.

"I'm sure you've told Sophia about the book," says my mother, trying to inject some life into the room. "She must be over the moon to be dating a creative director *and* an author!"

"*Executive* Creative Director," Louis chimes in with a piece of bacon in his mouth.

"She's been very encouraging," I lie.

Chloe, who has red wine spilled down her blouse, chimes in from across the table.

"I can barely finish *reading* a book, God help me if I ever tried to *write* one. Hey! You should get John Mulaney to do the audiobook now that he's out of rehab."

Louis furrows his eyebrows and wipes some beef fat from the corner of his lip before grilling me about the economics of the publishing industry.

"Walk me through how this works: You get an agent, he sells your manuscript to a publisher, they pay you an advance, and once the advance is earned out, you start earning royalties? Is that the deal?"

"Could be. I haven't really looked into it yet."

"It's not about the *money*, Louis," my mother interjects. "It's about making something you're *proud of*, something you can look back on and say 'I did that.'"

In reality, they're both wrong. I want to write a book because I have ideas that are special and unique and important—and they deserve to be admired by thousands, if not millions, of people. I want to elevate my social status beyond that of an Executive Creative Director at an "independent, global creative company." I deserve to be heard, understood, appreciated, respected, and remembered. I want people who don't have the discipline or ambition to write a novel to feel horribly insecure around me. I want women to be attracted to my intellect as much as they are to my body and my credit card.

Louis continues, unprovoked.

"I think the key with this is to cultivate a portfolio of IP, you know, *intellectual property*. The media landscape today is so fragmented. Think beyond paper and ink: movies, podcasts, merchandise, short-form video content, speaking gigs. You want the book to be the impetus behind a 360-degree franchise. *That's* where the real value is."

"You should consider a career as a literary agent if the mattress deal falls through," I say. I look at my thumb and see a streak of dried blood along the nail bed. I try to blot it on the inside of my Todd Snyder trouser pocket, but accidentally smudge some on my mom's white linen napkin. She'll know where it's from but pretend she doesn't.

"Have you ever thought about trying any of those creative writing classes they have in Hollywood?" Catherine asks.

"No," I say, disgusted.

"I heard most novels will be written by AI in ten years," she murmurs.

Brad juts into the conversation.

"You know what you need to do instead of taking some bullshit class? Meet my buddy, Duncan Friedland."

"That name doesn't ring a bell," I say, grateful that I don't have to answer any more questions.

"He's a published author. I think he's written seven or eight novels by now. His work is actually more popular in Europe than it is here. Anyway, Dunc was my fraternity brother, but he got kicked out sophomore year for selling cocaine to a TA. He was a hell of a writer, a natural, but he was about to flunk out. So he said fuck it, booked a one-way flight to France, and wandered around there for almost a decade, dead broke. Somehow, he managed to land a publishing deal, and that's been his hustle for the past thirty years. Now he lives somewhere up in The Valley. I still meet up with him every once in a while for drinks. Guy's a riot."

"And you think he could help me out?" I ask hungrily.

"I don't know what he can do. At the very least, you'll be entertained."

"Maybe I could meet him for lunch or something," I suggest half-heartedly.

"I'll put you guys in touch. Just a fair warning, he's a little on the...eccentric side. He's still holding out on getting a smartphone, drinks about a case of Diet Coke every day, and he's a socialist but also really into automatic weapons."

My dad speaks.

"What Brad's saying is that Duncan's a nut."

"You definitely won't find him at SoHo House," says Brad. "But give the guy credit—he managed to make a living just by putting words on paper. Pretty impressive if you ask me."

I don't want to disappoint Brad, so I tell him I'll meet Duncan at a restaurant of his choice sometime this week. I'm not hungry anymore, so I push my lukewarm beef around my plate with my fork to create the illusion that I ate more than I did.

When my mom goes to the kitchen to prepare crème brûlée and espresso, the conversation at the table shifts to *Succession*. Louis describes the show as "Seinfeldian," which is a term he stole from a review in *The New Yorker* earlier this week. Nobody asks about my book again.

On the way home, I shuffle Today's Hits—the first song is about a guy who doesn't want to sober up because he's having a lot of fun drinking with bad bitches at the club.

Meeting with Toothpaste Conglomerate

I'M FIDDLING WITH my Cartier Tank while a group of Executives from the Toothpaste Conglomerate file into the conference room. The agency flew them in from some bleak, third-tier city in Ohio for a 45-minute meeting so I can pitch three campaign ideas. KBM booked them at the SLS on La Cienega—probably the best hotel any of them will stay in for the rest of their lives.

Melissa Herschfeld, the hack I'm supposed to impress, plops into the chair across from me. She's the Conglomerate's Chief Marketing Officer: 54 years old, divorced, bachelor's degree from Michigan, MBA from Northwestern, total compensation hovering around $400K (including bonuses). She has the physique of a bulldog: thick-set and low-slung. Her pale skin, cratered with pockmarks, has a thick layer of sebum that glints under the LED lights. Her coffee-stained teeth could use a few months of Invisalign. Her T.J. Maxx trousers squeeze the blubber on her thighs like butcher's twine. She reeks of cheap perfume, like all the samples from JCPenney blended into one maddening olfactory assault.

"You either spend a lot of time in the sun or have unlimited access to a tanning salon," Melissa says jokingly with a faint lisp I can't unhear. "The weather here is fab, but I love my seasons in the Midwest."

"You have a point," I say, forcing myself to nod. "But I don't mind being spoiled."

Melissa is joined by the Conglomerate's Vice President of Marketing (an absurdly fit black guy in his thirties), Senior Media Planner (a frumpy woman with a bob haircut and no makeup who won't shut up about her cat, Brutus), and Director of Brand Marketing (a not-bad-looking blonde in her earlier thirties—I can't tell whether she's attractive, or if she just looks good by comparison to the human leftovers she came with).

As far as KBM goes, it's me, Brooke, Aaron, an art director named Alessio, and the VP, Scott Krause, who's probably plotting to replace me with his loser nephew in a few years. After everyone is seated, we pretend to enjoy the scalding hot coffee that was served in custom-branded KBM mugs while lobbing up softball topics to each other: the turbulence on the flight, the dense traffic, the interior redesign of our office, holiday travel plans. There's a pastry platter on the conference table, and Melissa gnaws hungrily on an apricot danish, leaving a trail of crumbs on her blouse while she rattles off a list of unimpressive universities her daughter is visiting this fall. I'm tempted to stress-eat a blueberry scone, but I resist because the sugar and carbohydrates will throw me off my game.

In theory, this meeting should mean nothing to me. I could tell these vitamin D-deficient slugs from Ohio to go fuck themselves, and nothing would change. I'd still wake up tomorrow and take the Porsche to have brunch at Destroyer. The stakes are nonexistent. And yet, there's a gnawing voice in my skull commanding me to make a grand impression on each and every one of these soulless corporate drones—to live up to the title of Executive Creative Director.

Brooke starts the meeting at 10 a.m. sharp, welcoming the Conglomerate's four clowns to Los Angeles. She's wearing a blouse that's one size too big, and I tilt my head to catch a glimpse of her bra through the gap between the top two buttons. Black, lace trim. I'm interrupted by my phone buzzing in my pocket, so I glance under the conference table. It's a call from a 213 area code. I send it to voicemail.

"I'll hand it over to our Executive Creative Director, Nathan, to kick things off," says Brooke.

I stand up from my chair at the head of the table and flash the fake smile I rehearsed in my mirror this morning. "Thank you, Brooke," I say, giving everyone just enough time to admire my outfit: a navy blue blazer by Ralph Lauren over a white button-down with light-wash jeans from Loro Piana. I start by regurgitating everything the Toothpaste Conglomerate told us when they sent their initial request for proposal, just in different wording. Corporate slaves love to hear their ideas and insights spit back to them because it makes them feel smart. I feel them lean in, starving for affirmation that their lives aren't a total waste of time.

I make eye contact with each person individually, explaining that today's young consumers are more socially conscious than their parents and grandparents, who mindlessly bought whatever toothpaste was on sale at their local supermarket. I stress that the young consumers we need to connect with aren't simply buying a tube of mint-flavored fluoride and calcium carbonate—they're buying the principles, values, and ethics of the company that puts their name on that tube. I emphasize that any toothpaste can scrub away stains and give your breath a minty-fresh sensation and decrease your risk of cavities—that's table stakes. They need a toothpaste that makes them feel superior to their less socially conscious peers. They need a toothpaste that makes them feel like they're part of something bigger than themselves. They need a toothpaste that will help them self-actualize. They need to find happiness inside that tube of toothpaste.

I use phrases like "disruption," "humanization," "social currency," and "behavioral residue." I tell them that "conversation is king, content is just something to talk about," which is a quote I read in *Adweek* a few minutes before this meeting. The words are devoid of substance, but I say them with enough conviction that they resonate anyway. I don't have any meaningful grasp on what's coming out of my mouth, but I have the whole conference room wrapped around my finger. I notice a few crumbs from the apricot danish are suspended by the fine brown hairs on Melissa Herschfeld's upper lip.

After the monologue, I pitch three campaign concepts, using Google Slides to reference visuals for each. First, a guilt trip about the devastating environmental impact of oral care products. Then, a charity stunt: underwriting free dental clinics in shitty neighborhoods. Lastly, a short film series about people who smile through war, poverty, hunger abuse, and other horrific life events. In conclusion, I stress that our target audience may be young, but they're not stupid. They can sniff out when a corporation hides behind a thin veil of altruism to sell products they don't need at a price they can't afford. But, I assure them, if we execute these campaigns to the potential that I know KBM is capable of, we can win their hearts, minds, and most importantly, that valuable space on their bathroom countertop.

Melissa nods with a kind of dopey reverence.

"I have to tell you, Nathan—as a matter of fact, I have to tell *all* of you—these ideas are right on the money. Y'all clearly dug into the research and worked your tails off to figure out what we need to get our brand out of this rut and back where it needs to be."

Krause exhales so loudly I can hear him from across the room. He has an immense, almost orgasmic sense of relief on his face.

"That's what we do best," I say with a perfectly symmetrical, pearly-white smile.

"I really love that Smile Equity concept," coos the absurdly fit VP of Marketing. "Powerful, powerful stuff in there."

"We knew to expect the best from KBM," says the not-bad-looking blonde Director of Brand Marketing, who has clearly become obsessed with me over the past half-hour. "But I can't remember ever being this excited to take an idea back to Cincinnati."

"Ditto," says Melissa, dusting a danish crumb from her blouse. "Now, one question I had was..."

And just like that, I shut down and tune out—it's up to Brooke and Krause to deal with any follow-ups. My brain drifts to a video I watched earlier about a guy who had his nose and nipples surgically removed. Then to a fantasy about a sloppy, aggressive blowjob from Lana. I make the rest of the minutes disappear by fidgeting with the Band-Aid on my left thumb—it's covering a small gash I inflicted on myself while lying in bed this morning, scrolling through headlines about a 17-year-old influencer who defrauded her followers with some cryptocurrency scheme.

As we exit the conference room, I watch a bead of sweat drip down Melissa's neck into her blouse. We shake hands, and as Brooke walks them to the elevator, I escape to the bathroom and check my phone.

News: Penis enlargement is on the rise—filler injectables are all the rage right now.

Emails: The shipment of my De'Longhi La Specialista Maestro Espresso Machine is delayed because of supply chain issues.

A missed call and a voicemail from a 213 area code. My thumb trembles as I press play.

"Hey Nathan, it's Duncan Friedland. Brad—you're uncle Brad—gave me your number. I guess you're too busy gallivanting around town to talk to an old fuck like me, but...ahh shit this motherfucker won't merge. Anyway, I'm busy tomorrow, but I can meet you for lunch on Thursday. If you're in, gimme a ring back."

Lunch with Duncan

I CALLED IT A DAY after an 11 a.m. meeting at KBM (which I left early), and I'm heading east on Olympic to meet Duncan Friedland for lunch at a deli I've never heard of in Westlake. I figured we'd go somewhere more dignified to discuss literature and the publishing business, like Baar Baar, the new Indian restaurant on 9th Street, for their monkfish osso buco. But Duncan didn't extend an invitation so much as bark out a time and location when I returned his call the other day, so my hands are tied.

Traffic is at a standstill because of a violent collision involving a school bus, so I'm passing the time by studying the billboards promoting new movies. All of them are remakes, prequels, and sequels of legacy franchises with rave reviews from news outlets I forgot existed.

As I approach a stoplight near MacArthur Park, there's a man with one leg crawling on the boiling pavement. He has an open wound about the size of a quarter on the thigh of his amputated leg, which I imagine is either a gunshot, an infected injection site, or some sort of flesh-eating disease. His arms are heavily tattooed with faded shapes and words I can't discern, but when I come to a full stop, I glance over through my Oliver Peoples sunglasses and see that the flesh on his arms is also covered with thick, raised scars that have hardened into a pink web-like pattern. A flyer nailed to a utility pole reads "JESUS SAVES." In the car, I'm mindlessly tapping my finger along to Today's Hits—the current song is about a guy who wants some of his girl's gushy-gushy because it's sweet, sticky, thick, and pretty.

I park the Porsche on 7th, max out the parking meter, and trot across the street, fleeing the stench of urine and body odor lingering on the sidewalk. Even though I'm five minutes early, I see Duncan is already standing on the corner smoking a cigarette, unbothered by the horror surrounding him. He looks vaguely like the pictures I saw when I Googled him. The long, rugged face with a layer of stubble. The furrowed brow. The intense frown. The deep-set green eyes, framed by black glasses. The curly brown hair cropped close to his head, now slightly more sparse and tinged with gray. He's wearing a plain, wrinkly, white T-shirt with a pair of blue jeans that are too short, and brown boots with frayed Kevlar laces.

I feel a pang of insecurity, worried that I'll come off as a pompous asshole since I'm wearing linen trousers by Brunello Cucinelli, a knit camp shirt by Sandro, and a new pair of Axel Arigato sneakers. The reality of the situation crystallizes in my head: We are different people from different times with different values and this could end up being a colossal waste of my time. But since there's a shred of hope that Duncan can help usher in my life's second act as a novelist, I adjust my sunglasses and make my way toward him.

"Duncan?" I ask, reaching out for a handshake. "Nathan Mansfield."

He has a hard, calloused grip, like he could change his own tire or fix a carburetor. We have a similar build, but it seems like he envelops my smooth, manicured hand.

"Glad you're an early," Duncan says, exhaling a cloud of smoke over his shoulder. His voice is deep and richly hoarse. "I'm fuckin' starving."

"Traffic was brutal," I say pointlessly, before adding, "I usually don't venture out this way."

He looks at my shirt, then my pants, then my shoes, then my shirt again.

"Did you come here to eat lunch or pose for *GQ*?" he asks with a blank look on his face. I can't decide whether he's an asshole or just trying to break the ice. Both, I conclude.

"*Vogue*, actually," I say, making sure not to sound offended.

Duncan chuckles under his breath, takes one last drag of a Marlboro Light, flicks it onto the sidewalk, puts it out with a scuffed boot.

The hostess seats us at a cracked pleather booth next to the window that looks out onto 7th Street. Outside, a woman with no teeth squats in the middle of the sidewalk and urinates, glancing from side to side like a nervous, neurotic animal. The laminated menus have pictures of the food, the ceiling tiles have piss-yellow stains, and our table is covered with a sticky film that's now on my fingertips. The air is thick and humid and smells like cured beef. Dishes clank in the background. I'm completely out of my element, nauseous and unsure how I'll be able to work up an appetite. I should be at The Rooftop restaurant at the Waldorf, but I refocus and remind myself that I need this meeting more than I need their new lobster burger with Gruyère cheese and green chili dressing.

"What's your story?" Duncan asks, not bothering to look up at me, eyes glued to his menu. I remind myself to sit upright with my shoulders back, as if good posture can compensate for desperation. Meanwhile, Duncan is slouching in the booth with the calm irreverence of someone with nothing to prove.

"How much did my uncle Brad tell you? I don't want to waste your time with the origin story."

"Apparently you're writing a book," says Duncan before snorting a glob of mucus from deep in his nasal passage. "Besides that, I'm out of the loop. Other than you're a Mansfield, so I know you won't be applying for food stamps anytime soon."

I feel my left eye twitch.

"Yeah, I started working on it a few weeks ago," I say, pretending his passive-aggressive comment didn't happen. "My novel."

"Give me the spiel."

I try to take a deep breath to steady my nerves. I stare at the glass of unfiltered tap water in front of me, desperately wishing it was filled to the brim with vodka.

"Yeah, so it's about this kid, this teenager, in high school who's desperate to get famous on the internet. And he commits a series of increasingly horrific and unspeakable acts to make that happen."

Duncan looks up from his menu for the first time since we sat down. I notice the white line of a scar above his left eyebrow. He nods, but I can't tell if he's nodding approvingly or if he's pretending to be polite.

"How far along are you?"

"A few thousand words," I lie, feeling my cheeks heat up. "I've been trying to get into the habit of writing every day. But it's not easy. You know, because of work and stuff."

"Writing isn't work?"

"You tell me."

"What's your gig?" Duncan asks after letting me suffer through an uncomfortably long pause.

"I work at an advertising agency," I say, before adding, "in Beverly Hills."

"That tracks. Copywriter?"

"Executive Creative Director," I correct him, quick enough to sound defensive.

"A thousand pardons," he deadpans. "Didn't know I was in the presence of royalty."

"It's not as glamorous as it sounds."

"It doesn't sound glamorous."

We sit in silence, staring at our comically large menus. I should ask Duncan a question about one of his books or follow up on a point he made in an interview. But I don't know shit about his work, except for the summaries I skimmed on Wikipedia when I was in line at Verve this morning. His magnum opus follows a paraplegic woman who stalks male celebrities in Manhattan in the 1990s. His breakout novel was about a priest in rural Missouri who develops a meth addiction and siphons money from the parish before fleeing to Mexico.

I start picking at a cuticle on my left ring finger until our waitress returns: a heavyset, middle-aged woman with a mole the size of a gumdrop on her cheek. Duncan orders a Diet Coke (no ice). I ask for a black coffee, which I immediately regret.

"You read much?" Duncan asks.

"A decent amount. More than most people, I'd say."

"That's not saying much. What are you into?"

"I like literary fiction, contemporary. Mostly satire, dark humor. I like Michel Houellebecq, Bret Easton Ellis— stuff like that."

"Is that why you're writing about a kid who wants to…what did you say, 'commit, horrific and unspeakable acts?'"

"Sure, I guess that style kind of inspires me, I guess."

"What do you read?"

"I love the Russians, man. Gogol, Nabokov, Pushkin."

"Dostoyevsky?"

"C'mon. That's a given."

"Is that who influenced you, the Russians?"

"What influenced me was being a degenerate who couldn't say no to a bottle of gin or a line of coke for two decades."

"I didn't know you were an addict."

"Still am one," he says shamelessly. "But I've been sober since 2001."

"How'd you manage to write so much if you were fucked up?"

He drinks nearly half of his Diet Coke in one swig, burps without opening his mouth, then blows it off to the side. I take a sip of coffee using my left hand because the nail bed on my right thumb is torn to shreds.

"I was desperate. My parents cut me off after I got kicked out of school. I had no real friends. I wanted to get the fuck away from everybody and everything, so I took the cash I had from selling weed and bought a one-way ticket to Paris. I thought that's where writers were supposed to live. I'd never tried to write a book before, but I was willing to fail. I was fine with being broke, I was shameless, and I had a high threshold for people thinking I was a scumbag. But I knew I had to figure my shit out somehow, otherwise I was gonna end up like that broad out there who was just pissing on the sidewalk."

I peer out to the sidewalk, where she's lying near the intersection in the fetal position, slamming her head against the base of a rusted trash can.

"How long did it take you to write your first book?"

"Six weeks, then I threw all 246 and a half pages into the Seine because it was dog shit. Then I started over."

Our waitress returns to take our orders. Before I say anything, Duncan asks for a pastrami and corned beef combo with a side of potato salad and another Diet Coke—no ice, he stresses. I panic and order a pastrami sandwich with coleslaw and Russian dressing. The couple next to us is discussing their dog's late-stage kidney cancer, which is apparently inoperable.

"Was it hard to bail on something you worked that hard on?"

"Nah, it felt incredible. It was the first time in my life that I accepted being a failure. Making a piece of shit is the best thing you can do to make something great. I couldn't articulate that when I was 21, but I felt it. I read the pages to myself, and I knew they were pathetic. So what was I supposed to do? Keep them under my bed as a souvenir? Show them to some broad and try to get laid? Why bother? They were garbage, so I treated them like garbage."

Duncan finishes the rest of his Diet Coke, making an audible slurping noise that draws the attention of the couple next to us, who are already visibly upset.

"So did you just start writing again the next day with the same idea?"

"I waited until I knew I had a real book inside me. It was probably three or four months before I started back up again."

"What did you do for money?"

"Didn't need it. I had some cash leftover from what I brought from LA. I met people in bars and slept on their couches. I ate leftover food that cafes were about to throw out and drank cheap wine. I borrowed books or stole them from libraries and sat around in parks and read all day. You don't need a salary and a benefits package to get by like that."

I take a sip of stale, boiling hot coffee and pretend it doesn't scorch my lips. Duncan grins at me.

"What? That make your perfectly moisturized, exfoliated skin crawl?"

"It just doesn't sound...conducive to a life of writing," I say, trying to dampen the combativeness in my voice.

"What kind of life do you think is conducive to writing?" Duncan asks, glaring at me. I'm terrified of the debate that I accidentally tripped into. I grip the coffee mug to steady myself.

"I feel like it would help to have some kind of...financial safety net. It seems like it would be hard to be creative if you didn't know where your next meal was coming from, or where you were going to sleep, or how you'd cover an emergency expense. I mean, you're in survival mode 24/7. Your brain doesn't have room to think."

Duncan wipes some condensation off his empty glass.

"You brought up Dostoevsky earlier."

"What about him?"

"He was an addict, too—a gambling addict. Roulette."

"That's what his book *The Gambler* is based on, right?"

"Yeah, but forget that. The story behind the book is better than what he wrote. He had been playing roulette in Germany, and after a week he dug himself into a deep fucking hole—something like eighty grand in today's dollars. It wasn't the first time this happened, and he was damn near about to go to debtors' prison. Not to mention, he was supposed to be taking care of his dead brother's family. Anyway, he was so desperate for cash that he bet some publisher he could finish a new novel in a year in exchange for getting his debts settled. If Dostoevsky didn't meet the deadline, he'd forfeit all the publishing rights and royalties to his past and future books for nine years. This motherfucker waited *eleven months* before he wrote a single word. Somehow, he finished *The Gambler* in 26 days and submitted it two hours before the deadline. A lot of people think Dostoevsky was some deranged piece of shit, and he probably was. But I also think he knew what he was doing."

"What do you mean?"

"I mean manufacturing a sense of urgency. It was either write the book or rot in prison and let his family starve. He figured out a way to hold his own feet to the fire. And it wasn't the only time he pulled that stunt, either. Pretty much every time he wrote a book, he'd take the money he made, go to a casino, and stay there until he gambled away his last penny. He said financial security made the act of creation pointless. So he impoverished himself over and over and over to reignite that flame that made him write. On his honeymoon, he spent five weeks in Baden-Baden and lost all his money again playing roulette. He and his wife roamed around Europe for years, dead broke. They pawned her wedding ring, earrings, and clothes to fund his gambling habit. She wrote poetry mocking him. It had to have been a miserable fucking life. But we wouldn't be sitting in this deli talking about him, 160 years later, if he was a well-adjusted gentleman who paid his taxes on time and picked up writing as a hobby."

The waitress carelessly tosses our food onto the table. I stare at the sad, slimy dill pickle next to my sandwich, piled high with ruby-red meat. My stomach feels like it's full of cement, but I have to eat so I don't embarrass myself. The waitress asks if we want anything else. Duncan asks for his third Diet Coke (no ice). She turns towards me, staring through a pair of burgundy cat-eye glasses, and I shake my head no.

"What I'm trying to say," says Duncan, gnawing hungrily on a mouthful of pastrami with Russian dressing smeared on his stubble, the muscles in his jaw clenching and unclenching. "What I'm trying to say is that pressure is an asset. We're wired to work under pressure. So if life turns into a cakewalk and everybody wants to suck your cock and pour champagne down your throat, the muscle that keeps you alive atrophies. You get soft and start decaying from the inside out—and people convince themselves that's a luxury. But if you put yourself up against a wall, you unlock this new gear you never knew you had."

"Because you have no other option," I say, absently.

"Look, I'm not saying everybody who wants to write a book should gamble away their life savings or pawn their wedding ring. But it's hard to sit down, day after fucking day, in front of a blank page and write words—hundreds of pages— with the odds of success or recognition close to zero when you can get rich selling marked up t-shirts made by child slaves in China or sending emails in an air-conditioned office."

"Is that a dig at me?" I ask, even though I know the answer.

He shrugs. "I don't have any idea how much money you

have—and no disrespect—I don't give a shit. But you got us onto the topic of safety nets, so I gave you my two cents."

We marinate in a long, uncomfortable pause.

"You saving your sandwich for later or what?" Duncan asks between bites of potato salad, gesturing at my plate with his mayonnaise-coated fork.

"I was just caught up in the story, I spaced out."

There's no dignified way to eat the sandwich in front of me. Too messy to hold in my hands. Too big to eat without unhinging my jaw. I coerce myself into biting off a chunk of fat-marbled pastrami and can't make my mind up to swallow it.

"Pretty good," I say, gnawing down mechanically.

"Best in the fuckin' city."

"How do you keep that same edge today that you had in your twenties?" I ask, trying to dislodge a caraway seed from between my molars. "Obviously you're not destitute—you have your shit together."

Duncan wipes his mouth with his forearm. Coughs.

"I can still taste the despair. I guess I have this subconscious fear that it could all fall apart. My books make enough for me to get by, but not enough to get ahead. So I don't delude myself. Every time I write, I put myself back at square one. I think back to where I was before I had a publisher, sleeping on some guy's floor in Rue Saint-Placide, stomach growling, without a dollar to my name. That idea that it could all evaporate tomorrow lights a fire under my ass."

Duncan, sensing I have nothing to say, continues.

"I think that's the problem when people with money want to start writing. In the back of their mind, they have an escape route, a crutch if things go to shit. Maybe it's some loaded relative who can bail them out. Maybe it's the idea that they have infinite time ahead of them. Or maybe it's a cushy job that's always there waiting in the wings. They tell you to count those things as blessings. But they're just mental pacifiers. If you have too many options, you'll never bet the house on anything. You have to get desperate to get anywhere."

I take a sip of lukewarm coffee, staring at my half-eaten pastrami sandwich, and grapple with the thought that Duncan is confirming what I already knew—that my upbringing, my income, my career, my relationships, my general lack of adversity—these things have obliterated my shot at creating anything worth reading. I consider saying this out loud for cathartic relief, but I'm too depressed to be vulnerable and too proud to admit it. So instead I just say, "Yeah, I don't necessarily disagree with that."

"I mean, look at John Kennedy Toole. Do you think he would've written *A Confederacy of Dunces* if he was chowing down on steak tartare and getting his balls licked in a cabana at the Four Seasons? The guy was a drunk, tormented professor, and publishers shit all over his work."

"And he killed himself."

"Ran a garden hose from his exhaust pipe in through the window of his car in Biloxi, Mississippi."

I chew, nod, swallow, wash it down with water. We sit in silence for probably 30 seconds.

"I have no idea if any of this is helpful," Duncan finally says. "I guess I should've asked you more about your book, given you some actual advice or whatever."

"No, it's been...instructive."

"Good. We'll do it again sometime."

Dominic Vaiana

For the remainder of lunch, Duncan tells stories about hookers he fucked in Paris and I just stare aimlessly at people inside the restaurant, many of whom are alone. I try to pay the bill with my Platinum American Express Card, but Duncan says, "Don't patronize me," hands the waitress a wad of wrinkled cash, and tells her to keep the change.

On the way home, I almost run over an elderly couple in Koreatown because I was glaring at a billboard announcing Post Malone's new algorithm gruel—a miserable plea for relevance that's destined to be a soundtrack for grocery stores and insurance commercials. I turn onto Melrose, where a crackhead is tweaking next to a bus stop ad that says "You Can Do Anything With a High School Diploma."

Shrink

"HOW'S THE NOVEL COMING ALONG?" Dr. Alper asks after 42 minutes of chitchat about the convenience of flying out of Burbank instead of LAX, the rapid uptick in gang violence throughout the city, and my recent decision to eliminate static stretching from my gym routine.

I slowly lower my head onto the back of the swivel chair, closing my eyes.

"Are you being sarcastic?" I ask.

"What makes you think that?"

"Never mind," I sigh.

"Last week, you mentioned how writing might be able to help you carve out an identity."

"Do we have to talk about this right now?" I ask, mildly annoyed.

"Not necessarily."

"Not *necessarily*?"

"It's your time, but I think it could be beneficial to unpack those thoughts if you're planning to devote a sizable chunk of your life to this project."

I wonder how Dr. Alper would react if I made myself cry really hard. Would he hand me a tissue? Stare at me until I stopped? If we ran out of time for the session, but I was wailing like a toddler, would he force me out of the room so the next patient could start their session on time?

"Did you know Dostoyevsky blew all his money every time he started writing a new book?" I ask.

Party at Bar Lis

"THE WHOLE POINT is that it restores a sense of...I guess I would say *harmony*," says Sophia, who's talking about the sound bath she took at a holistic wellness clinic in Malibu last week. Her one-hour session cost $450. "Like, it balances your physical, emotional, and mental systems and activates your body's natural self-healing system. But it can make you feel super emotional too. One girl literally cried—it was *so* beautiful."

Four women and a man—none of whom I know—nod intently between tiny sips from coupe glasses. As Sophia sounds off, I look helplessly around for a distraction. We're at Bar Lis to celebrate the launch of Dripsi, a direct-to-consumer brand of functional eye drops that are infused with CBD to "provide instant, calming relief in an era of endless screen time." They schemed their way into a million dollars of funding from a venture capital firm in San Francisco that invests exclusively in female-founded companies. Sophia met Dripsi's founder, Lorena Cho, at a Vinyasa yoga retreat in Joshua Tree last year. Apparently they've been in touch via Instagram.

"So do you, like, get *naked* for a sound bath?" one of the women asks half-jokingly, prompting everyone to giggle in unison. She's a blonde in her late twenties with an Australian accent—an algorithm's best guess for an LA transplant: aerobicized legs, a round, perky ass, naturally full C cups, no acne, just the right amount of lip filler. Sophia is too self-absorbed to realize I'm gawking at her.

"Oh no, don't worry, nobody's showing any skin," Sophia assures her with an insincere laugh. "They just call it that because you're being *bathed* in sound waves. Like, in my session, the instructor used a gong, chimes, and this metal bowl thing. Basically, the sound vibrations have different frequencies that heal your body. If you have an imbalance in any of your energy centers, the sound can reset those centers so energy can flow the right way."

"Wait, that's so cool," says the woman directly across from me. She's in a beige cutout bodysuit that shows off her nipples, which look rock hard because of the evening breeze. My eyes keep going there in quick, helpless glances.

"And the best part," Sophia continues, "is that you feel the effects instantly. It's not like other types of meditation where you have to do it for weeks or *months* to feel anything."

"You look *gorge*—it's giving Hailey Bieber," says the man in a voice so effeminate that it genuinely shocks me into paying attention. He's ethnically ambiguous and covered with lame tattoos that he probably copied from someone on Pinterest. I can't distinguish any of them, except for a grinning Buddha face on his right forearm. His outfit screams entry-level influencer with roommates and credit card debt: a blue pinstripe shirt (probably Zara) unbuttoned over a flimsy white tank, patent leather loafers (definitely Nordstrom Rack), and a Casio watch that someone convinced him was ironically cool. Even though it's pitch black outside, he's wearing slate gray Prada Symbole sunglasses. "If I wasn't a gay I'd fuck you on this couch right now, babe. Wait—this couch is so chic."

"*Stop*, you're so sweet. And yes, I do feel brand new. Honest to God, I do. My mood is better. My sleep score has been off the charts. Some, like, tummy issues I was having went away. Being able to find those small moments of stillness when everything is just so...I don't know *crazy* in the world— it's like a superpower."

Bar Lis is a French Riviera-inspired rooftop bar that looks straight out to the Hollywood sign. It's designed to capture the playful sophistication of Côte d'Azur. The space has a retractable roof, thirty full-grown cypress trees that line a 60-foot walkway, a ten-foot stone-finish water fountain, blue velvet banquettes, and striped pink-and-white settees. An impossibly tan couple poses for a picture at the bar. Nu-disco music plays in the background. Apparently Drake came here last month. The terrace is encased by plexiglass so people don't fall or jump off.

"I'm *literally* starving," says the Aussie.

"I saved all my calories for tonight," says Sophia, who draws a few laughs, but I know she's being serious.

"I don't really know if I'm hungry or not," says the woman in the see-through bodysuit. "But you know how if you *don't* eat for long enough you just, like, stop feeling hungry? That's me right now."

"That's me at work every day," says Sophia, unironically. "I skipped lunch so I could have the canapés here. I've been *dying* to try them."

"Ugh, we *love* a good canapé," says the Aussie.

"Am I supposed to know what a canapé is?" the effeminate man asks absently, looking vacantly towards something in the mountains.

"Frankie, it's a type of *hors d'oeuvre*, sweetheart," says Sophia.

"It's a piece of toasted bread," the Aussie chimes in, "and it's topped with something savory. They're itty-bitty and you eat them in one bite—like this."

"This girl I follow on TikTok said the smoked salmon one is *divine*," says Sophia.

I'm half-listening to this drivel as I dig away at a cuticle on my left thumb and read an article on my phone in *Bon Appétit* about how tinned fish are "in." Technically, the tins of fish are called "conservas." They can cost as much as $20 each, depending on where they ship from. Many grocery stores are running out of stock, the article says, because influencers are posting videos of their daily preparation and consumption of tinned sardines, mussels, and trout. They call it "hot girl food." I'm getting to the part about a chef in San Francisco who curates tinned fish date nights for $300 when Sophia tugs at my REISS canvas overshirt.

"*Nathan!* Off your phone, mister. Are you going to have another drink? Another...*Soleil?*" she asks, referring to the nearly-empty cocktail in my hand: Sipsmith gin, basil, passionfruit, Amaro Nonino, Angostura, house-made honey ginger syrup. I think it was $27, not including tax or tip. My tab is still open.

"Why not?" I sigh.

Our relationship has more or less stabilized since I skewered Sophia at Wally's about her lopsided life priorities. I told her that I'd be less hostile now that the Toothpaste Conglomerate campaign is off my plate and I can focus on my novel. She initiated makeup sex at my place last night. I got bored after about ten minutes and knew I wasn't going to come, so I ate her out while also using a $112 medical-grade silicone vibrator she read about in *New York Magazine*, which automatically cycles between 12 intensity levels.

"Gorgeous, I love that for you. Friends, are we ready for another round?"

The group marches to the bar where I promptly order a Don Julio 1942, neat. While I watch the bartender pour the tequila, I wonder how Sophia got us dragged here in the first place. Most of the people she calls "friends" aren't people she bonds with or even likes. They're just people she bumps into from time to time. But it seems like she's her element, which is good because it means she won't nag me.

"Nathan, have you met Ariana?" Sophia asks, gesturing to the woman in the see-through bodysuit. "She's about to launch the cutest denim line, and guess who she's partnering with…Sabrina *fucking* Carpenter. How incredible is that?"

"Nice," I say, nearly making the mistake of starting to care. "That's…impressive."

"You're making me blush," says Ariana, placing her hands over her chest.

"Hey!" Sophia gasps. "Maybe Nathan can help you with the advertising for the brand. You know he's the Executive Creative Director at KBM, right?"

I shut my eyes and instantly wish I had ordered a double Don Julio.

"KBN…" Ariana repeats, squinting her eyes and cocking her head.

"No, KB*M*," Sophia jumps in. "It's one of the best ad agencies in the country—in the world, actually."

"Oh, right! I thought it sounded familiar. My fiancée actually works in advertising, too. He's a VP at Ogilvy. We were living in Manhattan, but they transferred him out here this summer. He's down in Carlsbad golfing with some of his friends from Duke this weekend, otherwise he'd be here."

"Impressive, very cool," I murmur, making a mental note to look up VP salaries at Ogilvy later. "I'm sure you'll both love it out here."

"What sort of clients do you work with?" Ariana asks.

"Mostly CPG brands," I feel the words slur out of my mouth as I make a valiant effort not to stare at her nipples. "Toothpaste. Sneakers. We're pitching Cheez-It soon, I think."

"Oh my God, I haven't had Cheez-Its in *forever*," says the Aussie, who has apparently been eavesdropping. I notice she has a small, faint tattoo on the inside of her wrist that says E V O L V E. "I'd eat a whole *box* of the white cheddar ones right now if they weren't loaded with seed oils."

"Nathan hasn't mentioned the most exciting project he's working on, though," Sophia says, raising her eyebrows.

"Oooh, give us the tea!" Ariana beckons.

"I hope his project is telling our bartender to get a new haircut, because those sideburns are giving me the ick," says Frankie, disgusted.

I can't bring myself to say it, so I just stare into Sophia's eyes. Not angrily, just absently.

"He's writing a *novel*," she gushes, draping her arms around my shoulders and nestling her cheek into my chest. My initial reaction to this declaration is panic, which builds into a muted fury, before melting into an addictive sadness. The word count on my novel is stalled at 96.

"Ahhh, we're in the presence of an *author*," the Aussie purrs. "The last of a dying breed, some would say."

"You're not wrong about that." I take a gulp of my Don Julio 1942, desperate to narcotize myself.

Dominic Vaiana

"So, can you tell us what it's about?" Ariana asks in a
tone that comes off as daring. At this point, my only option is
to get obliterated. I toss back the remainder of my tequila,
embarrassed by how quickly I've finished it. I feel the alcohol
burn away my inhibitions, and I'm overcome with this urgent
impulse to validate not just my idea, but my whole identity to
Ariana—a woman I need to manipulate into believing I'm
important.

Although the rational part of me knows Ariana only
asked about my book as a formality, I can't stop myself from
spewing a lengthy, aimless monologue about the novel I've
allegedly been writing for the past six weeks. But after about
ten seconds, it registers that I haven't thought it out to the
degree that I could articulate it, even if I were sober. And yet
my drunkenness emboldens me to speak louder, with gusto,
making up obscure scenes and subplots and characters (for
some reason, I mention a detective named Brett McCollum).
And what makes all of this more embarrassing is how
authoritatively I'm speaking. I abruptly conclude with a vague
suggestion of a murder-suicide, and as I place my lips on my
glass (which I realize is empty), it clicks how absurd I must
have sounded. The whole thing was preposterous—an
indisputably lame performance. And now the group is
paralyzed by boredom, their eyes glazed over, cringing as they
attempt to muster a polite response.

"That sounds very, uh, *zeitgeisty*," says Frankie.

"Yeah, very...of-the-now," Ariana adds.

My palms are breaking out in a cold sweat. My face is
melting.

"Nathan had a meeting with a big-time writer the other day to talk about, you know, *writerly* stuff," says Sophia, oblivious to my anguish.

"Is it somebody I would know?" asks Ariana.

"Duncan Friedland," I say. "He's popular in Europe."

"Hmm, he doesn't sound familiar. But I'm just a BookTok girlie," she giggles.

"Have you heard of Martin DuVall?" Ariana asks. "He wrote *Feral Symphony*, that new book about the queer subway rat. Literally everyone's reading it. It made me bawl my eyes out, but I couldn't put it down. It's just so...well, I can't do it justice. You just have to read it for yourself."

"Can confirm," says Frankie, snapping his fingers. "Marty is a fucking icon."

"I'm trying to do more creating than consuming right now," I stammer, immediately realizing how pretentious I must sound.

"I think he's doing a live reading at Book Soup next month," says Ariana. "We should all go!"

"Gorgeous," Sophia says. "And we can go to Cipriani for a bev after."

"Are you repped?" the Aussie asks out of nowhere.

"What?" I ask, glancing over my shoulder. I thought I heard someone laughing at me.

"Repped, like, do you have an agent?"

"Not yet," I say, wondering if I should have lied. "I want to have the full manuscript ready before I start shopping it around."

"My brother works in literary at UTA—I can *totally* put you in touch when you're ready."

"Nice, yeah, for sure," I say, making sure my gaze doesn't go below Ariana's neck. "That would be...cool."

"Soph, remind me to send you Sage's contact info so you can give it to Nathan when he finishes writing his book."

"Of course, babe. Look at us, making connections!"

Next to us, I overhear two women debating whether their friend should check herself into rehab for a Ketamine problem.

"My man looks *delicious* tonight," Sophia says, slurring slightly while lunging toward me with her red lips puckered.

"You know my stance on PDA," I say, sternly.

"Just a quick smooch! I promise I don't have cooties."

We smooch, quickly.

"Those girly pops are sweet, right?" Sophia says, while taking a pill I don't recognize. "It's so funny because we all follow each other on Instagram, but it's the first time any of us have actually hung out in person." She washes the pill down with the diluted cocktail in her rocks glass.

"Yeah, they're...cool people."

"Speaking of cool people, I was talking to one of the photographers when we first got here because I wanted to know where she got her pumps. She was so sweet and *gorgeous*.

I wish I had her tits. And she's only 24—such a *baby*. It turns out her family is friends with Lorena Cho's family because they're all from Scottsdale, and that's how she got invited to shoot tonight. Such a small *world*. I think her name was Layla...no, *Lana*."

My palms break out in a cold sweat. My heartbeat crashes into my ears. My vision narrows as the terrace wobbles under my feet. I'm on the verge of a breakdown. It can't be

Lana, my Lana. She should be at home, sending me soapy shower selfies or setting her allowance on fire at a resort in Cabo—not wasting her Saturday night snapping photos of social climbers at Bar Lis. All of the possible scenarios start unfolding in my head:

Fake a migraine so I can leave the party early and drag Sophia with me.

Corner Lana and come clean about having a girlfriend.

Spend the rest of the night making sure they don't run into each other again.

Do nothing.

I reluctantly commit to the last option. These girls aren't Nobel Prize contenders. But in case they figure out that they've been sharing my dick, the situation could actually work out in my favor in the long run. Sophia would immediately dump me, fast-tracking a decision I've been working up the balls to make for months. Lana would block me, and I'd desperately miss the sex. But I'd have one less distraction pulling my attention away from writing.

"What's wrong, babe?" Sophia asks, tugging at my sleeve. She sounds far away, like she's underwater. "Hellooooo?"

"Sorry, I...thought I saw someone. I think I'm going to get another drink."

"Oh, fab! I'm ready for one too. I really liked that *Mon Chéri* I had earlier, the one with the rhubarb liqueur."

"You want that again?"

"Should I do something else?" she asks, oblivious to my anguish. "A spritz, maybe? No, no. I should stick to vodka, otherwise my tummy will hurt, right?"

"Totally."

As I wave my Platinum American Express at the bartender, I notice Sophia and her friends are speaking in hushed tones, muting their facial expressions, and darting their eyes back and forth.

"Is that Cassandra *Mancini*?" Ariana asks.

"One hundred percent, without a doubt that's her," says Sophia.

"She's the one who directed that movie where the quadriplegic boy falls in love with his therapist?"

"Yes, that's the one where she cast an actual homeless fentanyl addict."

"I thought she'd be hotter in person."

"*No one* is hotter in person," says Frankie. "That's a fact."

"And she's a writer-director?"

"I think she's a director-*producer*."

"No, she's a *writer-producer*."

Cassandra Mancini is unremarkable in the looks department. Short and wavy auburn hair (possibly dyed), clear but pale skin, flat-chested, neither fit nor fat. She's wearing a Loro Piana blouse, black pants, and black ankle-strap shoes—understated yet sophisticated. She struts toward the antique water fountain and poses for a picture with an actor I recognize from an HBO drama, but I'm too drunk to place him.

I'm about to order our drinks when the woman leaning up against the bar catches my eye, tinkering with the settings of a Canon camera. Her tits make me double-take. It's Lana, my pool mistress, and I can tell by her pumps that she's definitely the photographer Sophia ran into. I spin up a fantasy of a threesome at The Maybourne, but the bartender snaps me out of it.

"What can I get for you, man?"

"Oh, yeah."

"What are you having?"

"A Mon Chéri and a...do you have any skin contact wine?"

"We have Orange Gold."

"Where's that from?"

"I believe it's from France."

"I'll do the Faiveley Bourgogne Pinot Noir—a glass of that and the Mon Chéri."

As I look out across the terrace at Bar Lis, I see everything I hate about myself, but deep down know I still am. People who fill the hellish void in their lives with marked up booze and cheap conversations. People who pride themselves on authenticity, but couldn't, with a loaded gun to their temple, articulate an idea that hasn't already been implanted in their brain via an iPhone. Cultural parasites. People who adopt a new personality every year because they never bothered to cultivate one of their own. People who crave a connection to a world that disgusts them. People who will be forgotten. Zeroes. People who are rewarded for parading around their most despicable qualities. People whose perception of reality has been warped beyond recognition. People who cringe at the idea of responsibility. People who will drunk drive back to custom-designed homes, fuck each other's brains out, come over and over again, and wonder why they don't feel anything. People who are deranged, delusional, and damaged beyond repair.

Two drinks are waiting for me on the ledge of the bar. I blunt whatever feelings I have left in my head with a gulp of

Pinot Noir before handing Sophia her *Mon Chéri*. She looks into my eyes, waiting for me to say something. I have nothing.

"I'm glad we worked things out," she finally says. "I don't like it when we fight."

"Yeah, life's better without conflict."

"Life's better with a...what's this? A *Mon Chéri*," she says with an exaggerated fake French accent, clearly drunk and unaware of the double entendre.

"I'll be right back."

"Okay, you go find the little boys' room. I'm going to find Lorena—I haven't even talked to her tonight."

"Who?"

"Lorena *Cho*, the whole reason we're here tonight, silly."

"Right," I say as Sophia lays a boozy kiss on my cheek. I amble toward the restroom, nearly tripping over a woman's Jimmy Choo combat boots. Lana and I catch eyes for a fraction of a second. Neither of us says anything, but I can tell by the dead, empty look in her blue eyes that our summer fling is over.

Shrink

I'VE SPENT 53 OF MY 60 MINUTES with Dr. Alper rehashing a childhood memory of my dad berating me for accidentally shattering one of his Josephinenhütte wine glasses, which he received as a wedding gift from my grandfather. I was pouring apple juice into it, pretending to bartend at my French restaurant in the foyer, when I knocked it onto the hardwood floor. I think I was seven. My dad said it wasn't the broken glass he was angry about—that could always be replaced. He was angry because I should've known better than to be so careless with something so special to him.

"And what are the 'wine glasses' of his that you're breaking today, as an adult?" asks Dr. Alper.

Martin DuVall's Digital Footprint

AFTER A SOLO DINNER at Osteria Mozza, I force myself to sit down at my Jean Prouvé desk and forge ahead on my novel for the first time in eight days. I pour two fingers of Blanton's, put my phone on Do Not Disturb, strap on my AirPods Max, queue up a two-hour playlist of Mozart's greatest works, and settle into my chair like a surgeon preparing to examine something horrific.

I'm trying to get in the zone, but instead I have a flashback of getting sucked into conversation with a self-proclaimed screenwriter at a cocktail party at NeueHouse—some insufferable software geek who wouldn't shut up about his "edgy" pilot script that stalled out somewhere between thought and act three. The idea that I'm on the same path—impotent ambition, all talk, no follow-through—makes me shudder, so I open the Google Doc titled "Chapter 1."

I know the word count before I even look, but I check anyway, pointlessly hoping it would have crossed the three-digit threshold by now. I can't remember where I left off with the opening scene, so I brace myself with a sip of whiskey and reread the two short paragraphs I have so far, hoping I'm not totally mortified.

The narrator, a 15-year-old boy, sits in the back of his parents' Volvo watching a video of two pranksters smoking cigarettes and pushing a stroller with a fake baby through a busy intersection. Pedestrians freak out because they think the doll is a real infant. The narrator explains that he's not watching the video to entertain himself, but to study its structure so he can replicate the formula for his own channel.

I feel the buzz from my whiskey, Mozart's Piano Concerto No. 20 in D Minor twinkling faintly in my ears. I start typing something about the narrator arguing with his parents about his 2.1 GPA. I envision him as the polar opposite of the kid I was at 15: disrespectful, allergic to authority, impulsive, undisciplined. I reread everything from the top. My writing is structurally and grammatically flawless—not a typo in sight or a comma out of place. But it reeks of inauthenticity, of fraudulence. It's too sterile, too clinical. The scene that was so vivid in my head morphed into something muddy and weak on the screen. It reads like something a high school student in an AP English class armed with a thesaurus would hammer out if he were desperate to pad his GPA.

The most infuriating part is that there's nothing I can do—no formula, no blueprint to polish these three shitty paragraphs. If you're a fat pig, you can starve yourself and run on a treadmill until the number on the scale dips. If you want to make beef Wellington, you can go on YouTube and have someone hold your hand through the whole recipe. I don't have any fucking clue how to write a sentence that makes someone want to read the next one and the one after that for hundreds of pages. The writers I idolize make their work seem effortless, like they were born with some supernatural talent. Or maybe, like Duncan told me, it's something that only comes to you when you're desperate, so intensely hungry that you have no choice but to figure it out. I think back to his story about throwing all 246 pages of his manuscript into a river because he knew it was all shit. I picture myself printing out my lone page of work, crumpling it up, and throwing it into the Pacific Ocean. It paralyzes me with fear.

I open a new tab and Google "what percentage of manuscripts get published?" One percent. Everyone else's precious story vanishes into the digital abyss. My knee-jerk reaction is that I could self-publish, but deep down, I'd know that was more pathetic than not writing the book at all. I'd be consigned to the same realm of desperation as SoundCloud rappers and comedians who upload their standup specials to YouTube, spewing mediocrity into the void. And who would forfeit six hours of their life to read it? My mom? Sophia's brain-dead friends? Felix? A few stray hate-readers?

Thirsty for a new motivating force, I Google "Martin DuVall author." In the same way watching an obese slob ride a motorized wheelchair into a Taco Bell compels me to show up to the gym every day, I want this self-righteous keyboard warrior to light some creative spark deep within me, piss me off enough to become America's Houellebecq. Or at least something. DuVall's face pops up immediately—paper-white skin that's never seen the sun, emaciated face, unbearably smug grin, beady eyes, an frizzy mop of sandy-blonde hair brushing over a pair of oversized black-framed glasses. On the right-hand side of the screen, his bio:

Martin DuVall is an American author currently living in Brooklyn, New York. In 2024, DuVall published his debut novel, *Feral Symphony*, which the *New York Times* heralded as compassionate, fierce, and seductively original. He holds an MFA in Creative Writing from NYU. Born: 1996 (age 27 years)."

I click on his personal website, a minimalist design plastered with blurbs from every newspaper and magazine that still pretends to matter. I click "About" and skim the highlights: born in Providence, Rhode Island, bachelor's degree in history from Sarah Lawrence College, shortlisted for a bunch of awards I've never heard of, editor of a digital literary journal called paperWERK, lives with his cat named Luna.

I click "Contact," which brings up the email addresses of his publicist, speaking agent, film agent, and literary agent. Below this list is a form to send "fan mail." Over the next half hour, I furiously type (and delete) six different messages that range in tone from critical to illegal. One sarcastically congratulating him on getting into a liberal arts college with a 5o% acceptance rate; another providing a detailed set of instructions for how to kill himself by using a garden hose to asphyxiate himself with a vehicle's exhaust.

As the buzz from my whiskey dissipates, the anger I had hoped might turn into fuel melts into a sterile apathy. I stare out of my window onto the golf course of the Los Angeles Country Club, waiting for a breakthrough that I know won't occur. Every few minutes, I change the font size of my manuscript or play around with the margins and line spacing so that the words take up more space on the page. But I mostly just stare at the blinking cursor and fantasize about what I can access on my iMac within a matter of seconds: the new cashmere collection from Brunello Cucinelli, real-time stock prices, *GQ*'s new list of the world's most stunning hotels, the nudes Lana sent before our fling ended, delivery services that will send yellowtail sashimi and Cabernet Franc to my apartment, beheading videos, my bank account. Not to mention virtually unlimited pornography. I recently read an article that said nearly 15 terabytes of sucking and fucking are uploaded to Pornhub every day, the equivalent of half of Netflix's entire content library.

I check my newest word count: 189. I convince myself this is a reasonable stopping point. I knock back the rest of my whiskey, close the Google Doc, and reward myself by masturbating to a video of two Latina women initiating a three-way with an unsuspecting male taxi driver. I ejaculate weakly and stand under my rainfall shower head, scrubbing myself with Molton Brown Dark Leather shower gel until the hot water runs out. To fall asleep, I prop my phone against a pillow and watch a video with nine million views where a guy goes to the worst-reviewed chiropractor in New York, but I doze off before I can see what happens.

Lunch at the Polo Lounge

IN TOKYO there's a 34-year-old man who just fulfilled his lifelong dream of transforming into a Bernese Mountain dog. The headline was kind of misleading—he didn't "transform" into a Bernese Mountain dog, per se. He paid a costume company to make a hyper-realistic suit, complete with actual fur, which took 38 days to create and cost more than $14,000. The man documented his transformation on his YouTube channel, which has more than 50,000 subscribers, and his "coming out" video amassed 4.2 million views in less than a week. Now he uploads videos of himself doing tricks, sniffing real canines in public parks, and eating dog food out of a metal bowl. Despite being proud of his transformation, the man is extremely careful to conceal his second life as a dog from family and friends, using a pseudonym for the content he posts online. "I haven't told anyone about my transformation into a dog," he tells the reporter. "I am very afraid that my friends will think my hobby is bizarre." Adding to his stress, the man is getting an overwhelming amount of hate mail from strangers on the internet, many of whom are suggesting that he kill himself.

It's 10:53 a.m. and I'm reading this story at my desk at KBM while I mindlessly peel off the cuticle behind the nail of my right ring finger. I can see the mutilated skin underneath, and even though I can feel my finger throbbing with blood, the pain is overshadowed by a vague sense of comfort. On the news website's "You May Also Like" column, there are stories about a 14-year-old rapper in Orlando who faked her own death, a stripper in New Orleans who fell in love with a face transplant survivor, and a Filipino man who had a dental procedure to lengthen his two front teeth so he could look like a rabbit. As I'm deciding which one of these to click on and waste three more minutes, Brooke, Aaron, Alessio, and Krause bounce into my office, smiling maniacally.

"Did you see the email?" Brooke asks, all giddy.

"Umm, which one?" I say, pretending to look intently at my screen. "I've been...doing some research on Cheez-Its."

"Melissa got back to us this morning—they gave us the green light on the Smile Equity campaign idea! We kick off next week!" Last night I closed my eyes and pretended I was fucking Brooke while Sophia was bent over my kitchen island. I thought my fantasies would get even more intense when I saw Brooke today, but her enthusiasm for something as meaningless as an exploitative campaign for a Toothpaste Conglomerate eviscerates my libido.

"That's great," I say, forcing myself to smile.

"This is a huge milestone for the agency," Krause says, deadly serious. "Blue chip brand, national campaign, massive budget. I know you don't like tooting your own horn, so I'll do it for you. We couldn't have done it without you, Nathan."

"Well, it was a team effort," I say, folding my hands on top of my desk. "Everyone deserves credit."

"Spare us the canned corporate bullshit," says Aaron, putting a nicotine pouch behind his lower lip. "Can we go get fucked up somewhere and celebrate?"

"Remind me again why we hired you," says Krause, only half-sarcastically.

"I'm just saying what everyone else is thinking."

"It's not even *eleven o'clock* yet," says Brooke, checking her Apple Watch.

"I could be persuaded into a boozy lunch," I say, kicking my Oliver Cabell sneakers up onto my desk.

"The Executive Creative Director has spoken," says Aaron.

"Fuck it, I'm in too," says Krause. "Where do we want to go?"

"How about that new pizza place in WeHo?" Brooke asks. "The one with the cute little patio and the..."

"Negative," says Aaron, cutting her off. "This isn't fifth grade. We're not having a fucking pizza party to celebrate a fat contract with the biggest toothpaste brand in the world. "

"*Second* biggest," Brooke corrects him.

"Whatever. Nate, you're the LA restaurant czar. What's the game plan?"

"Sounds like KBM's picking up the tab, so my vote is the Polo Lounge."

Before we leave, I bookmark the article about the stripper who fell in love with the face transplant survivor.

I don't want to have lunch at the Polo Lounge because of the food (almost everything on the menu is offensively mediocre, the chocolate soufflé notwithstanding) or because celebrities loiter there (there's nothing more pathetic than being star-struck by people who secretly lust for attention). I want to go to the Polo Lounge because it's brutally honest about what it is: a garish, gaudy playground to waste large sums of money in public.

Dominic Vaiana

Unlike the restaurants approved by influencers and adored by normies, the Polo Lounge doesn't pretend to be accessible, approachable, or relatable. It's a shrine to opulence and excess. It is a stage as much as it is a restaurant—a place where you're not only allowed but encouraged to flaunt your wealth without being made to feel guilty. Toss the valet a hundred-dollar bill to keep your G-Wagon out front because you can't be bothered to wait four minutes. Keep your $1,500 sunglasses on in the dim indoor dining room. Demand an obscure, off-the-menu cocktail and tell the waiter you had it last time—even though it's not true. Behave like a coddled animal.

In 2014, a bunch of entertainment juggernauts like Jeffrey Katzenberg, Jay Leno, Ellen DeGeneres, and Elton John staged a moralistic boycott of the Polo Lounge after its owner, the Sultan of Brunei, imposed Shariah law in his country, making gay sex and adultery punishable by stoning. That lasted about five minutes before the restaurant bounced back as the premier power lunch spot for actors, agents, producers, and string-pullers to make deals over crab cakes and martinis.

Millions of people are still repulsed by the Polo Lounge—or at least the idea of it. Self-proclaimed food snobs wouldn't be caught dead eating a McCarthy Salad. Last week, some failed journalist wrote a 400-word screed, whining that the food was "designed for wannabe Hollywood people with no teeth or ability to taste" and warning readers they would leave "miserable, hungry, and broke."

I'm sure she'd happily choke down a bowl of their tortilla soup if it meant she'd never have to blog in a rent-controlled studio to pay off her student loans.

Los Angeles may be saturated with cash — old, new, and foreign. But there's a growing sentiment of disgust toward luxury and a fetishization of the working class, especially among twenty-somethings. Whether they managed to scrape up some money on their own or had it wired to them from a concerned parent, I've met countless people who hate themselves for being rich. They parade around Melrose or Los Feliz dressed like paupers, wearing frayed carpenter pants, tattered fatigue jackets, and stained trucker hats for jobs that require them to sit in a climate-controlled box and press keys on a computer. They cosplay as impoverished artists and unionized laborers to give their lives a veneer of grit despite cringing at the idea of responsibility. They pretend to hate money because they know it defines them.

What's nice about the Polo Lounge is how honest it is about its inauthenticity. Located in the Beverly Hills Hotel, where rooms start at $1,200 a night, it is comically pretentious and insultingly expensive. They make it painfully clear that normal people off the street don't belong here. It is a giant middle finger to humility, hard work, and discipline — and that's exactly what I want right now.

The maître d' seats us at a table in the bar area (I would have preferred a booth, ideally Booth One, which is strategically placed to give a panoramic view of the space). A pianist twinkles out "What a Wonderful World," temporarily dulling the aching hopelessness I've felt since I woke up this morning.

Some of the guests here are attractive, most of them are dressed well, and all of them seem bored. I look through the retractable windows out to the patio, where an Asian couple is seated under an umbrella, taking pictures of a salad. At the bar, a woman in her late sixties sits alone with a Bloody Mary, reading *Vogue* through a pair of Gucci butterfly sunglasses. Her hand shakes slightly as she raises the glass to her lips and sets it back down. Jason Bateman and his wife are next to us, nibbling on crudités. Brooke won't stop staring. As I'm tapping through Lana's latest Instagram story—a mirror selfie at the gym followed by a filtered shot of her new nails positioned to show the Range Rover emblem on her steering wheel—a server in a white suit jacket swoops in to take our beverage orders.

"Two bottles of Dom Pérignon," I say before anyone else orders.

"Absolutely, sir," says the waiter. "And for you, miss?"

"I'll just have…" Brooke stalls, deliberating. "May I just have a Diet Coke?"

Aaron looks up from the bread basket. "Did I just stroke out, or did you really order a DC?"

"You guys enjoy yourself," she says, blushing. "I'm just…not in the mood to drink right now."

"Not even for a glass of Dom?" asks Alessio, shocked.

"How about a spritz?" asks Krause, genuinely concerned. "They do an excellent spritz here."

"Yes, the Polo Patio Spritz is a classic," the waiter assures us.

"I'm really fine…I'm going for a long run tomorrow morning at six," says Brooke. "Trying to stay tuned up for the charity 10K I'm running next month."

"Does anybody want to guess where I *won't* be tomorrow at six?" Alessio groans, rolling his eyes.

"Well, the bar is open all day in case you change your mind," says the waiter, smiling through his misery.

"Bring an extra champagne glass just in case," says Krause. "And I know it's early, but I'll do a two-finger pour of Pappy Van Winkle," says Krause. "Ten-year."

"You got it, sir."

"Actually, make it the twelve-year."

"Of course."

Alessio orders a cocktail called "Think Pink." Aaron orders one called "The Millionaire." I realize I'm still wearing my Jacques Marie Mage aviator sunglasses, so I set them on the table as I listen to the three of them ramble on about the Smile Equity campaign—how it will elevate KBM's status and how the agency can parlay this into more work with the Toothpaste Conglomerate and other Fortune 500 corporations. Meanwhile, I'm thinking about potential titles for my novel and what I might want the cover to look like—a design that's simple but shocking. Something that will send the publisher's legal department into a frenzy.

I order appetizers for the table: truffle fries ($28), fried calamari ($37), shrimp cocktail ($35), and a half dozen oysters ($31). For my main entree, I get the American Wagyu Burger ($46) and the McCarthy Salad ($43). Our food arrives promptly, and it's immediately clear why the Polo Lounge hasn't won any culinary awards. One critic called the food "an affront to human decency." Another called for it to "be shut down until the chef wants to start taking food seriously." I'd never admit it out loud, but they're spot on.

Over the next hour and a half, I down five glasses of champagne to anesthetize my tastebuds. I would've had a sixth, but Alessio poured himself a glass after he abandoned his El Jardin Gimlet after he realized it had jalapeño in it, which irritates his canker sores. The alcohol triggers an irresistible craving for sugar, so I order a chocolate soufflé, which Brooke stares at enviously, and wash it down with a shot of espresso. Krause picks up the tab, which is some obscene amount, and I'm glad I won't be the one who has to take shit from Accounts Payable.

"So we're calling it a day, right?" Aaron asks.

"Consider it part of your bonus," Krause murmurs, signing the check.

"I think I'm going to head back to the office for a little bit, just to catch up on some email," says Brooke.

"Martyr," Aaron mutters.

I drive home with my vision going in and out of focus, without a doubt over the legal limit. Once I get to the stoplight at Bedford and Santa Monica, I text Sophia to let her know I cancelled the dinner we were supposed to have at some new Parisian brasserie in Culver City (even though they have a duck confit with Valois sauce that got rave reviews in *Los Angeles Magazine*).

It's only 2:45, so I have the rest of the afternoon and evening to make some serious progress on my novel. Instead, I get caught up watching a reality show on Netflix that follows six people with Down syndrome as they navigate the trials and triumphs of dating.

Shooting My Shot After Workout Class

I WAKE UP AT 5:57 A.M., surprisingly refreshed even though I slept with a stomach full of champagne. It's the last Tuesday of the month, so the first thing I do is use my Face ID to unlock my Citigold Private Client Checking Account. The $45,000 deposit from my trust is there, as it is every month, with the memo "DOMESTIC WIRE TRANSFER." Seeing those five digits gives me a sense of relief, followed by something that might be called gratitude, which then fades into a diluted mixture of boredom and guilt. It takes about thirty seconds to cycle through these feelings while I change into my workout clothes, which arrived the other day from Alo.

I booked a spot at the Full-Body Bootcamp at tempus this morning. According to my app, it can burn up to 700 calories with its combination of cardio and strength training. I rarely attend fitness classes—mainly because the instructors are insufferable failures, but also because I'm in such better shape than everybody else and it's not as challenging as I need it to be to maintain my physique. But I try to drop into the Full-Body Bootcamp once a month because there's an absolute specimen named Emilia who attends religiously, and if I don't try to lure her back to my apartment I won't be able to stop fantasizing about her while I'm having sex with Sophia. As far as I can tell from Emilia's Instagram (12K followers, which is a little suspicious), she's single or at least hiding a boyfriend she's too embarrassed to hard launch. More Dominic Vaiana

importantly, Emilia doesn't have any mutuals with Sophia, so I'm in the clear to shoot my shot after class.

I rinse my hair in the sink, pat it dry with a microfiber towel, and add just enough Ishi Sculpt Texturizing Hair Pomade to hold it in place during my workout, but not so much that it looks overly-styled or formal. I study my fingers in the soft bathroom light. They look okay, aside from two small scabs along the nail bed of my left thumb and right ring finger. I'm craving a goji berry smoothie from the cafe downstairs, but I pass because I read that exercising in a fasted state can ease cognitive stress throughout the day, which I need since I haven't taken my Effexor in weeks.

I drop my Porsche off at the valet at tempus at 6:40, stow my Louis Vuitton duffle in the locker room, and head up to the Group Fitness Studio. A moderately attractive Vietnamese girl, who I'm pretty sure is in love with me, checks me in with an iPad. Emilia is in her usual spot in the rear left corner of the room. I try to catch her eye while I grab a towel and fiddle with my water bottle, but she's glued to her phone, the screen casting a cold, artificial glow over her blank expression. I'm not sure what her ethnicity is but it's something exotic—could be Tahitian or Lebanese or Native American. She has curly brown hair and hazel eyes and dimples and a birthmark above the left side of her lip. No tattoos, at least none that I can see. Her B cups aren't exactly the star of the show, but they're perfectly round and proportional to the rest of her body, plumped and pressed together by a black sports bra from SET. She's wearing a pair of high-waisted biker shorts, which accentuate an ass that no other woman could sculpt with any amount of Glute Blasters, high-protein diets, or plastic surgery—she's a genetic lottery

174

winner. I position myself close enough to be in her line of sight, but far enough to not seem desperate.

The Bootcamp is divided into ten-minute blocks, alternating between free weights, resistance bands, and running on the treadmills. The instructor, Josiah, a 34-year-old failed actor from Wisconsin, barks encouraging sound bites into a microphone headset at random points throughout the class: *You got this. Dig deep. You can do it. Don't quit now.* At the same time, he's deejaying the class with trap remixes of 5o Cent's "Candy Shop" and Travis Scott's "SICKO MODE." A pudgy, red-faced girl next to me stops every two minutes to catch her breath and guzzle something out of a Stanley Cup (probably some sugar-loaded sports drink that she thinks is hydrating her). She's obviously more embarrassed than exhausted.

I glide through the 45 minutes with ease, working up a light sweat in the process, catching myself in the mirror, deltoids and calves glistening. We finish with a cool-down mobility circuit and a light stretch to bring our heart rates back to resting. Josiah's tone shifts from boisterous to monk-like, instructing us to "send gratitude to our strong bodies" and "let go of whatever doesn't serve us." The attendees, drenched with sweat, clap and high-five each other as if they just scaled Everest while I look over my shoulder to make sure Emilia doesn't make a mad dash. As everyone files out, I spot her standing alone at the towel shelf, tapping at something on her Apple Watch.

"I like your HOKAs," I say cooly, gesturing to her white and copper shoes with my Hydro Flask. "Almost bought a pair yesterday."

She glances up and the expression on her face is surprised but not necessarily enthused.

"Oh!" she says, looking down at the ground as if she forgot what she was even wearing. "I love these. I got them when I was training for my half marathon, but they're great for workouts like this too."

"More importantly, they match your SET outfit. I'm Nathan," I say, extending my hand and surprising myself with a natural smile.

"Emilia, nice to meet you." Her teeth are blindingly white, impossibly straight—a cosmetic dentist's wet dream.

"I see you in here all the time—figured I was overdue for an introduction."

"Oh yeah! I'm here, like, pretty much every day," she says, sneaking a glance at her phone.

"Do you pay extra to reserve that spot in the back every week?"

This gets a chuckle. I'm in.

"I would if I could. I just try to show up early before someone steals it."

"I'll warn the others not to encroach," I say, instinctively flexing my abs even though she can't see them.

"Appreciate you looking out for me."

My heart pounds and I can feel my window closing.

"I know I'll see you here again next Tuesday, but maybe I can catch you before then—ideally somewhere other than a room full of sweat and treadmills."

A hesitant giggle.

"I um," she looks off to the side, but nothing's there. "I'm actually seeing someone."

My fingertips turn cold and my stomach turns into an empty pit. I instinctively glance from side to side, making sure nobody heard me get rejected. The only person within earshot is the fat, red-faced girl mopping her puddle of sad, disgusting sweat off the floor. Not a threat. I proceed.

"I can't say I'm surprised to hear that."

"Yeah, sorry," she says, making this deal-with-it face.

"No need to apologize," I say, wiping a bead of non-existent sweat from my brow. "I'll see you around. Nice to meet you."

"You too! And what was your name again? Sorry."

"Nathan."

I give her a pathetic wave goodbye. As I watch Emilia walk away, I persuade myself that the birthmark above her lip is gross and that she's probably wearing makeup to cover acne and that her boobs actually aren't proportional to her ass and that her voice is too masculine and that she's probably ran through anyway.

I hunker down in the sauna, cringing as I replay every syllable of my failed conversation with Emilia in my head. I can't stand the silence so I step into the shower, letting the cold water punish me before I check my phone. I scroll through my notifications—six emails from Brooke about the Toothpaste Conglomerate, three Instagram Reels Sophia shared with me, a reminder about my HydraFacial tomorrow— and then my chest tightens when I see a missed call and voicemail from Duncan. I lift my phone to my ear.

"Nathan—Duncan Friedland. I know you're probably busy duping innocent people into buying shit they don't need, but let's grab lunch sometime this week and shoot the shit. I know we didn't talk much

about your book last time, so do me a favor and send over your manuscript and I'll try to give you some feedback, or something close to it. Duncfriedland63 at Gmail. Catch you later."

I'm standing naked at my locker, paralyzed by a full-body sense of doom and on the verge of a breakdown. This is a big problem, an unmanageable problem, since the current word count of my novel is 189. At our last lunch, I told him I had written a few thousand words. By now, he probably expects me to have at least doubled that. He actually used the word "manuscript"—not "a few pages" or "what you have," but "manuscript." As in something that resembles a full-length book.

As I stare helplessly at my phone, my brain starts feeding me a highlight reel of all the hours I've wasted over the past six weeks: narcotizing myself with disaster porn, Googling symptoms of diseases I know I don't have, buying new versions of clothes I already own—an ambient haze of indecision and curated distractions. I pry a cuticle near my thumb with surgical intensity, blood pooling in a clean, neat dot on my nailbed. A small and perfect punishment.

I'm too embarrassed to call Duncan back so I send him a text instead: *"Not ready to share the manuscript yet, long story…let's still meet Thursday at noon if you're free."*

Second Lunch with Duncan

"WHAT HAVE YOU BEEN UP TO, MAN? Savoring the fruits of your leisure?" Duncan asks sardonically, twirling a splintered chopstick between his index and ring fingers.

"Good one," I murmur.

"You have my blessing to steal it. Pitch it for one of your next campaigns."

"I need all the help I can get."

We're on the second floor of a strip mall inside a Chinese restaurant that can only be described as grim: dense, humid air that reeks of refined vegetable oil, tile floors with a permanent film of grease, harsh fluorescent lights, an empty jar with "TIPS" scribbled on white tape, employees with surgical masks. Across from us, a middle-aged man sits alone, slurping wonton soup while watching news from some foreign country on his phone, which is propped up against a bottle of soy sauce. I grab my plastic cup of water and feel the condensation soak the Band-Aid on my thumb. The combination of shame and guilt and discomfort makes me so desperate for alcohol that I have to make a conscious effort to stop my hands from trembling.

"So, what's up with your book?" Duncan asks. "You scared of the red ink?"

"Nah," I say, trying to simulate a tone of confidence. "I can handle that."

"Then why are you holding out on me?"

Dominic Vaiana

I helplessly glance around the restaurant, unable to make eye contact with Duncan, before looking down at the table.

"I—I, uh, deleted the whole thing," I lie, hearing myself sound like a bad actor in a school play. This is the story I concocted last night while alone and four martinis deep at Honor Bar. I figured telling Duncan I scrapped the book (just like Duncan did with the first book he tried to write) would be more respectable than admitting I squandered the past month and a half drinking myself into oblivion, chasing pussy, and letting my phone drip-feed me digital poison.

"You deleted the whole thing," he says. It sounds more like a statement than a question.

"Yeah, it's gone for good."

"And why'd you do that?"

"It was a piece of shit," I say, hoping I sound as serious as I intended to. Duncan scratches his beard with both hands.

"It's never as bad as you think," he says insincerely.

"I can assure you it was fucking awful."

Duncan sighs.

"I wasn't aware I had to remind you, but you're not gonna win a Pulitzer the first time you put your ass in a seat and write."

"It was a lost cause," I murmur, as the cashier starts barking on the phone in what I assume is Mandarin.

"You gonna start over?" Duncan asks after an unbearably long pause.

"Yeah, probably," I say, feeling my hands suddenly get cold. "Maybe. I don't know. I need some time to think it over, I guess. But that's why I still wanted to meet with you today— to make sure I'm in the right headspace."

Whatever little patience Duncan had evaporates from his eyes. Something tells me this will be the last time he's willing to put up with my bullshit. We sit in silence for what feels like hours before an emaciated waitress comes to the table with a quiet look of desperation in her eyes. Duncan orders Kung Pao Beef and his second Diet Coke (no ice). I realize I haven't even looked at the colossal, laminated menu, so I choose something at random from the lunch specials page: sweet and sour chicken.

"I'm gonna ask you a question," says Duncan, leaning forward.

"Shoot."

"Do you want to write or do you want to be a writer?"

"What's the difference?" I ask, realizing I sound annoyed.

He tosses back the rest of his Diet Coke before leaning back and crossing his arms.

"I've lost track of how many people I've met who typed the words 'Chapter One' on their computer, but they all fall into one of two camps. You have the ones who love the process. It's torture, but they crave it. They can sit there for hours, lost in whatever world they're spinning up. You can't pay them to do shit else. They're maniacs driven by some divine force. And then you have the ones who get giddy at the idea of 'writer' as an identity—a personal brand, as you might call it. But they hate the process. It scares the shit out of them. They don't want to write—they want to have written. Their wet dream is telling some broad at a cocktail party that they have a novel or screenplay so they can score a blowjob or a free drink."

I open my mouth and hope something half-intelligent oozes out to fill the silence, but I just sit there, slack-jawed.

"You and I both know why you started that book. You wanted to prove you could make something happen on your own. Anybody with a pulse could've sniffed that out. All your life, people chalked up big asterisks next to everything you've got—your fancy job, your girlfriend, that shiny Porsche you double parked in front of that fire hydrant out there—because your last name is Mansfield. So you cooked up a plan to prove them wrong by reinventing yourself. But the fucked up reality is that writing a book won't change what anybody says about you behind your back, or to your face. As a matter of fact, it'll probably reinforce it."

There's nothing I can say that wouldn't make me look worse, so I let Duncan continue his rebuke.

"Did you think somebody would have an epiphany and say 'Wow, Nathan's such a brilliant, disciplined genius?' No, they'll say your dad bribed an agent or called in a favor from one of his golf buddies. If you're going to spend months, years cranking this thing out—and I know this sounds like some corny Mister Rogers shit—do it for yourself, not for some girl you're trying to fuck or some asshole you want to feel insecure."

A bitter taste floods my mouth as I nod slowly and severely, like I imagine I would if someone told me that a close relative died. This is the first time anyone has so quickly and effortlessly cut to the core of my worthlessness. Each word felt like a razor cut across my undefended ego. I don't know whether to lash out, leave quietly, or just sit here like a toddler who got scolded. I notice my hand start to tremble.

"I didn't delete it," I say after a deafening silence, staring at my empty water cup.

"I know you didn't," Duncan says coolly.

For a second I feel like I might actually cry, but I blink twice and clench my fists to hold in the tears.

"I have to finish it," I say in a voice I don't recognize, miserably aware of how desperate I must sound. "I told my girlfriend, I told my parents, I told all these random fucking people. I'll quit my job if I have to. I'll go off the grid. I..."

"If you want it that bad, you'll make it happen," Duncan says bluntly. "The best advice I can give you is to raise the stakes—put some skin in the game. The best writers I ever knew were too busy to worry about money. You'd be surprised how much hardship you can stomach when your reputation's on the line."

Our Styrofoam plates arrive and Duncan immediately digs into a heaping mound of Kung Pao Beef, which steams and glistens under the harsh fluorescent lights. I stare at my plate of sweet and sour chicken and try to think of the last time I willingly ordered something so grotesque. I'm embarrassed to be in a restaurant this repulsive. I'm embarrassed to be embarrassed. But this is the crux of my problem: The fact that I give a fuck about eating sugar-coated chicken in a strip mall instead of eating lobster ceviche in Malibu confirms how pathetic—how inconceivably vapid—my life is and always has been. I have no hunger, no desperation. No real problems to solve, no obstacles to overcome. Just a never-ending series of traps that I set for myself—a catatonic joyride insured by a multi-million-dollar financial safety net that will always be there to save me.

Dominic Vaiana

Before the pause becomes uncomfortably long, I pick up a chunk of chicken with my splintered chopsticks. The hot, rubbery meat is drenched in a thick, sickly-sweet concoction of sugar and vinegar that assaults my taste buds. I can actually feel a headache creeping in as I chew it.

Over the next half hour, Duncan and I swap stories about traveling in Europe. His stories are radically different from mine—gritty, depraved, hilarious, sad. I guess that's because he writes, and I want to be a writer.

Shrink

AS I EXIT INTO THE LOBBY of Dr. Alper's office, there's a man in his forties whose pale face has been frozen into a state of expressionlessness by decades of Botox. Perpetually raised eyebrows, shiny forehead, swollen cheeks—a grotesque parody of youth. He's wearing black Saint Laurent sunglasses and he keeps puffing on a vape cartridge that smells like peppermint. A copy of *GQ* with Paul Mescal on the cover sits open on his lap; but he's just scrolling on his phone, stopping every few seconds to pull it unnervingly close to his face before breaking into these weird, guttural laughs.

As I'm pushing through the door, I hear him say loudly, to no one in particular, "It's all happening again, isn't it?" in this weirdly flat tone—like it's both an accusation and a joke I don't understand.

I drive to the CVS at the corner of Beverwil and Pico to pick up a box of Band-Aids. I keep my Matsuda sunglasses on so nobody recognizes me. On the way out, I buy the latest issue of *Men's Health* and a bottle of oxygen-infused water before heading home to watch the series premiere of a new reality show about the lives of geriatric porn stars.

Dinner with Sophia at Maude

"SO, I KNOW WE HAVE THE AIRBNB in Topanga booked for next month," Sophia says, wiping a drop of achiote sauce from the corner of her lip with a linen napkin, "But Celeste and Felix texted me this morning—they have two extra tickets to the Benson Boone concert and I told them we'd think about it."

"You know I hate concerts," I say, trying to decide whether I like the leather bomber jacket this Persian guy in the booth across from us is wearing.

"Ugh," she says, rolling her eyes, "I just don't get you sometimes. Watching live music is the most *magical* thing you can do, it's like an out-of-body experience."

"It's not the music that bothers me, it's the audience's enjoyment of it."

"What does that even *mean?*" Sophia asks, exasperated.

"Never mind. I think we're about to land the Cheez-It account, so my hands are going to be tied over the next few weeks either way."

I've been distant tonight because I decided that I'm finally going to dump Sophia. She hasn't done anything wrong—at least nothing she hasn't already done since we met—but I've sold myself on the idea that I'll finally be able to dial into working on my novel if I cut her out of my life. The endless social obligations, the lengthy date nights that only end in sex half the time, the relentless ping of her texts, FaceTimes, and DMs—none of it is conducive to the life of a writer. I'm not sure exactly how or when during the meal I'll break things off (ideally, I'll find a window of opportunity around the dessert course), and I've made peace with the fact that I'll trigger some sort of public mental breakdown. But when it's all said and done I'll walk out of this restaurant a single man, ready to reinvent myself.

"Babe, you know how important quality time is for me...for *us*," she says, as my attention drifts toward the half-eaten quail leg on my vintage floral plate. We're on the home stretch of a nine-course tasting menu at Maude, a shoe box of a restaurant off South Beverly. Maude earned a Michelin star for its focus on refined Southern Californian cuisine, which the *Los Angeles Times* called "a love letter to the Golden Coast with a touch of obsessive-compulsive disorder."

I didn't tell Sophia, but my first time at Maude was with another woman last year—a failed actress from London who ended up making over $300,000 selling videos of herself showering on OnlyFans. I'm not usually a restaurant repeater, but I watched an interview with Maude's new *chef de cuisine* who's placing a big emphasis on his Sinaloan upbringing along with seasonal ingredients, and it seemed worth another go. Our prix-fixe tasting menu, with a Reserve Wine Pairing, costs $420 per person. The dishes are transgressive, but not too far out of my comfort zone—the Nixta pasta with huitlacoche is one of the better things I've tasted this fall, although it's a little salty.

"Yeah," I say, knocking back the remainder of my Jean Grivot Pinot Noir. "So many people underestimate the importance of quality time."

"Well, we can talk about it tomorrow. It's okay. Hey, do you think this quail is a little... *salty?*"

As I watch Sophia delicately chew the quail, I wonder if I'm about to make a terrible, irreversible mistake. Granted,

Dominic Vaiana

I'm two and a half glasses of wine deep. But I notice her eyes seem more intelligent and alive, her face more expressive, her lips fuller, her curves more exaggerated, her cleavage more pronounced. She did something different with her hair, too, something sexy, but I can't tell exactly what it is. Not to mention, her outfits have been meticulously curated recently. Tonight she's in a slinky dress from The Attico with Stuart Weitzman pumps and diamond earrings from Material Good. This is always how it seems to go when I'm on the verge of ending a relationship or even a fling. I get this sense that the woman is subconsciously taunting me, daring me to find someone with better tits, better taste, better in bed. And maybe that's the point—that I can't.

For the last portion of the meal, our waiter escorts us out of the building and upstairs to Maude's private pastry room, complete with plush armchairs, a vinyl record collection, and a 3,000-bottle wine collection. I take a deep breath, catching whiffs of leather, caramelized sugar, and espresso. There are two middle-aged couples up here as well as a group of four clearly gay men who keep eyeing my Berluti Capri Leather Boots. "Too Late to Turn Back Now" by Cornelius Brothers & Sister Rose plays on a turntable. Sophia, comfortably buzzed, embarrasses me by doing a little twist-dance to it.

After hanging on by a thread to a conversation about her coworker who's having vision problems after starting Ozempic, our dessert arrives: garam masala carrot cake, orange blossom ice cream, and some type of candy with a truffle filling. I'm going to need more alcohol if I'm going to follow through with my plan, so I flag down the waiter and ask for a Germain Robin XO brandy, neat.

"Do you ever think how lucky we are," Sophia says, though not in the form of a question, sipping out of a tiny vintage teacup. "We're young, healthy, successful, eating *literally* maybe the best food you can get on the planet. Not to be cringe, but we really are...blessed? Lucky? And we get to do it all *together*."

"About that," I say, wiping a nonexistent scuff off my boot.

"About...what?" she says with a nervous giggle.

"Together." The way I say this gives away everything. My face is on fire, my tongue feels like sandpaper. "I've thought about this a lot, and you're a mature woman, so I'm sure you'll understand."

Her face is layered with some expensive combination of foundation and blush, but I know that underneath it her color is draining rapidly.

"You're not..." she says, and I notice her hand start to shake before she hides it under the table.

"I have a lot of weaknesses, I can admit that. But my biggest weakness right now is that I can't focus on my book. And I think what I need to do is...pare down the things in my life that are distracting me. At least for a while."

"What the fuck does *that* mean?" she hisses. "You want to *break up*? You want to break up *here*?"

"I think we need to, yeah," I say gravely, glancing at her half-eaten carrot cake.

"I can't tell if you're being serious or not. What did I do? Fuck, I'm starting to sweat," she says, fanning herself with both hands.

"It's nothing you did or didn't do. It's just...where I'm at in life right now with my goals. I need changes."

"What goals? What *changes*?" she says, gesturing wildly at nothing.

I uncross my legs and lean in to show my sincerity, then speak slowly yet assertively—a hollow, bureaucratic edict: "This is what's going to happen over the next several months: I'm going to spend a lot more time writing, seriously writing, and that's going to cut into the time we spend together. At first, I told myself I could make time for this, for you. But I know I'd be distant and irritable, like I've been recently. And I know that would hurt you. And you'd tell me to take it easy, to not take my work so seriously because you're not feeling validated. And that would be perfectly justified from your perspective, but it's not what I need right now. Actually, I'd need the opposite advice. I'd need you to tell me to spend more time alone, to get rid of every last distraction. And from there, it's just going to spiral out of control and get ugly and toxic. And you'd resent me. So instead of dragging you through that kind of mess, I'd rather just make a clean break. Does that make sense?"

I can actually see her pulse intensifying under her Cartier necklace.

"That's the dumbest fucking thing I've ever heard in my entire life," she says, her anxiety now replaced with vitriol. I notice her hand is still shaking a little bit.

"Is it? Or is it the best decision I'll ever make?"

"You can't write a book and be in a relationship at the same time? Those are mutually inclusive?"

"Mutually *exclusive*," I correct her. "And maybe not all relationships, but our relationship, yes. I don't feel propelled toward greatness when I'm with you. I feel weighed down by the expectations that you've set, or that we've set. The dinner dates, the gallery openings, the weekend getaways, the insufferable lunatics we waste time with. None of it is conducive to creativity."

"You're a literal *child*," she says, raising her voice and furrowing her eyebrows. By now, everyone in the private pastry room can tell something is wrong, and I can see them murmuring to each other.

"I don't want you to think I'm using my book as an excuse to get rid of you. There are other changes I'm making, too. I'm also—and I trust this will stay between us—I'm also probably going to..." I pause, taking a glance around. "I'm probably going to ask my parents to remove me from the trust."

The expression on her face changes from one of anger to one of confusion and, almost, sympathy.

"You're losing your *fucking mind*, do you know that?"

"I've never felt real pain. I've never been desperate. I've never felt isolated. I've never had to grit my teeth. I've never had to fight or claw or scratch. And it's made me soft. Mommy and daddy's money has always been there to bail me out. I live in a Nerf world with Nerf problems and Nerf people. And that's why I've never accomplished shit. Why bother? What's the fucking point of trying? Nobody's lighting a fire under my ass, so I'll just do it myself. Otherwise, I'm going to waste the prime of my life at fucking KBM, making shit up to sell toothpaste and Cheez-Its."

"Well, I'm glad you had your little awakening, or whatever this is," she says loudly and sarcastically. "Thanks a lot for wasting the past eight months of my life."

She flings her napkin onto the table and stuffs her phone into her clutch.

"Jesus Christ, Sophia, don't make a scene."

"Fuck you. And fuck your book."

The waiter scurries over to our table.

"Hi, folks, sorry to interrupt. I'm going to have to ask you to keep it down."

"He'll take the check whenever you're ready," says Sophia, her voice shaking with rage.

"Very well," says the waiter, clearly disturbed.

Sophia's Stuart Weitzman pumps clack on the wood floor as she stomps out. I drove tonight, so I'm guessing she'll take an Uber home. While the waiter prepares the check, I take a piece of Sophia's garam masala carrot cake off her plate, my first bite of food as a single man. For some reason, it doesn't taste as good as I expected.

Letter to My Parents

I'M JOLTED AWAKE at 6:03 a.m. by a violent hangover, courtesy of Maude's Reserve Wine Pairing and the glass of gin I poured myself after I got home. My stomach is convulsing and it feels like someone is splitting my skull open with an ice pick. I forgot to drink my electrolyte supplement before bed because I got caught up watching near-death experiences on YouTube until I passed out in the Aimé Leon Dore leisure shirt I wore to dinner.

I reach for my phone, expecting a text from Sophia—either a guilt-drenched thesis on the irrevocable mistake I've made, or a sentimental Hail Mary begging me to reconsider. But the only notifications I have are about a software update that's going to be installed on my phone tonight and a few news headlines:

Gangs of child thieves are targeting bars across New York City.

Self-checkout kiosks may be making Americans lonelier.

Elderly women are taking up pole dancing as a new form of exercise.

The blue light from the screen intensifies the pounding inside my head, but I'd rather embrace the pain than sit alone with my thoughts, so I just stare at the back of my eyelids, willing the time to pass by faster. Despite feeling half-dead, I'm swept by my usual hangover horniness, so I fetch my MacBook Air and pleasure myself with a dab of Aesop Hand

Dominic Vaiana

Balm—first to a video of two blonde women who take turns eating each other out at a pool, then briefly to a Japanese woman who fucks her personal trainer through a pair of torn spandex shorts while balancing on a medicine ball, and finish myself off to a scene where a freckled brunette rides a guy's dick while a skinny blonde girl sits on his face. I ejaculate weakly, a few dribbles of watery semen that pool on my bronze abs. It feels like a chore. I clean myself off in the shower, turning the knob to get the water as hot as possible. As I lather myself with my Molton Brown Dark Leather shower gel, I count my abs, the only fruits of my labor I have to my name.

After toweling off, I amble to the kitchen and force myself to chug a quart of Evian water from my refrigerator, which triggers a churn in my stomach so intense that I have to grip the counter to stop myself from puking. It's 6:49 and I stand naked staring at my bookshelf in the living room, realizing there's literally nothing for me to do today except trudge away at my novel. This fills me with a sense of existential dread that I'm not ready to face, so I start picking at my cuticles, which are still tender and pliable from the shower's steam. Time slows down as I dig and pull and tear at the fragments of weak flesh until the layer of tender skin below reveals itself.

As I study the blood under my fingernails, the morning sun illuminating my apartment, I hear Duncan taunting me. I hear Sophia and her gang of girly pops cackling at me. I hear Felix sarcastically asking me for an advance copy. I hear Dr. Alper analyzing me. I hear my mom and dad shamefully whispering their concerns to each other. I hear Martin Duvall pontificate about the joys of filling a blank page every day. I hear Lana and Ariana and Kendal Behkar asking if I can read my work aloud to them in bed. These voices melt into some grotesque, distorted wailing noise, and it becomes immediately clear that I have to invent a crisis for myself if I ever want to make it go away.

I rinse the blood from underneath my fingernails before slipping into a pair of French terry Alo shorts and my new linen t-shirt from Sandro. I'm ready to pour my heart and soul onto a Google Doc, but I feel an intense craving for caffeine as soon as I rest my hand on the mouse, so I go back to the kitchen to brew a cup of coffee.

Lately, I've been making coffee with a Chemex using the pour-over method. I grind my beans—single-origin, Sidama Region, Ethiopia. While the grinder works, I boil some Mountain Valley Spring Water in my gooseneck kettle. Once it hits 205°F, I rinse the filter to get rid of the papery aftertaste. Ten grams of ground coffee go into the preheated carafe. I bloom the grounds in a slow pour—center outward. After thirty seconds, I do three more concentric pours, evenly spaced, until the kettle is empty and the apartment smells like Community Goods, minus the crowd of clout leeches.

Watching the coffee trickle into the carafe, I try to summon the motivation to be creative, to express myself, to toil and labor and slog it out—but it's not there. Or maybe the motivation is there, but locked in some kind of glass box where it's visible but inaccessible. I'm not sure how to unlock it, but it's probably something I don't have the balls to do. Maybe being diagnosed with a terminal illness or getting blackmailed would snap me into focus. But as things stand, I'll coast through the prime of my life, wasted at parties I don't remember, hollowing out my brain with digital slop, fucking women who mistake my boredom for mystery, and hemorrhaging money on toys I don't want to impress people I resent. It's so tempting to blame all of this on my parents, who sheltered me from obstacles that build character, handed me treasures that I conflated with success, and gave me a life that was defined by more certainty than doubt.

I pour the coffee into a ceramic mug I ordered from an artisan in Kyoto. It's made using a technique that absorbs bitter catechins and releases umami. I carry it carefully back to my desk, making sure not to spill any coffee on the white oak floors. But instead of opening my manuscript, my hand veers and I start typing a new document, almost unconsciously:

Dear Mom and Dad,

First, I want to thank you both for the opportunities and support you have provided throughout my life, particularly through the Mansfield Family Trust. Your generosity has allowed me to experience things most people never will.

Recently, I've reflected on the trust fund's impact on my personal and professional development, especially as it relates to my interest in becoming a writer. While the security it offers is immense, I'm beginning to understand that it's also interfering with my ability to develop discipline, self-sufficiency, and motivation. That's why I'm formally requesting to be removed as a beneficiary of the Mansfield Family Trust.

I understand that this decision will come as a surprise. However, I want to assure you that this isn't a rejection of your support, but rather a step toward reclaiming a sense of purpose and autonomy.

I'm open to working with you and our attorney(s) to navigate my removal from the Trust in a way that's fair and appropriate. Please let me know how we can proceed.

Sincerely,
Nathan

It's the most words I've written in one sitting since college. For a moment, I feel liberated imagining my parents' reaction, huddled over their iPad in their newly remodeled kitchen. My mom, dumbfounded, would call Dr. Alper and demand that he up my Effexor dosage. My dad, more offended than confused, would view the decision as a personal affront. I get a perverse sense of comfort picturing them feud about what they did wrong, whose fault it is, how they can sway me back, how they'll spin it for the rest of the family. I take a sip of my coffee which has gone lukewarm—I must have lost track of time.

I read the letter back to myself again, delete all of the text, and drag the document into the trash icon on my MacBook.

Shrink

"DREAMS CAN BE powerful mirrors of our emotions," Dr. Alper tells me as I press my thumb against the inside of my pocket to stop the bleeding. I kept my Cutler and Gross sunglasses on for this session because there's a really bad glare in the office, which is being amplified by a mild hangover and a poor night's sleep. "What stands out to you the most about this dream in particular?"

Dr. Alper has been trying to get me to keep a dream journal. Something about "excavating my unconscious self," "unlocking new insights into how I'm processing fear," and "reclaiming hope." I'm supposed to scribble down everything from my dreams on a notepad as soon as I wake up, but I can rarely recall them. The only ones I remember are sexual fantasies about random women I see throughout the day—a 19-year-old barista with an underbite, the Mexican girl mopping the floor at Erewhon, a woman at a bus stop eating Takis.

Instead, I've just been making up gruesome, outrageous stories to gauge Dr. Alper's reaction, but more so to make the time go by faster. I come up with them while I wait in the lobby before my sessions, rehearsing the monologue like I'm auditioning for some part I don't want.

Last week, I "dreamed" that I drove a truck full of kittens to Manhattan Beach and drowned them in the ocean, one by one, while a crowd of old men in tuxedos cheered me on from the shore. The week before that, I took a chainsaw into a Build-A-Bear workshop at the Westfield Century City mall and beheaded a bunch of stuffed animals while screaming the chorus of "Wonderwall" by Oasis. Today, I'm recalling a "dream" in which I knocked out all of my teeth with a sledgehammer and shipped them to my parents' house with a note that said, "I hope this hurts you more than it hurt me." A few times, I made Dr. Alper grimace, but mostly he just sits there with his legs crossed, nodding along.

"Do you notice any patterns or symbols from this dream that you might want to explore?" he asks in a tone so even it makes me want to snap the glasses on his weaselly little face.

"If I had a gun to my head, I'd say it's connected to my fear of being punished for speaking out to my parents when I was a kid."

Dr. Alper rests his chin on his fist.

"There's only one person in this room who has the power to punish you right now, and it's not me."

Fall in Los Angeles

I SPEND THE REST of the fall in a stupor, mostly in my office deleting unread emails, booking reservations at new restaurants that I almost always end up canceling, going to the gym at odd hours and staring at myself in the mirrors without working out, trolling Martin DuVall's Instagram with the burner accounts I made, or wasting entire days on my couch, mindlessly watching YouTube shorts while *Seinfeld* reruns play on my new 70-inch OLED TV in the background. The days slip by obliquely, with little worth mentioning. I can identify and conceptualize various emotions that float into my head, but I can't really feel them. Nothing seems real—I'm trapped in a gruesome echo chamber of the self, haunted by the sonics of my wounded ego.

I just subscribed to an 18-year-old Canadian YouTuber who's documenting his journey eating raw steak for 100 days in a row—it's better than anything Netflix has put out in months. I bought some books on Amazon after reading an article titled "49 Books Every Aspiring Male Novelist Needs On His Shelf," including *Crime and Punishment*, *Nicomachean Ethics*, *The Complete Short Stories of Ernest Hemingway*, and a first edition of *No Country for Old Men*. I can't make it past the first ten pages of any of them, so they're stacked on my Hervé van der Straeten coffee table, next to a miniature Bonsai tree that keeps dying.

My Smile Equity campaign for the Toothpaste Conglomerate failed so badly that they pulled it after one day because the stock tanked five percent. *Ad Age* called it a "cautionary tale about faux-wokeness." *The Atlantic* skewered it as "the deadliest misstep a brand has made this decade."

Still, KBM managed to win the Cheez-It account. My campaign idea that the client selected was a Cheez-It-themed rest stop halfway between LA and Indio. Here, festivalgoers will be able to replace standard car fuel with "snack fuel," delivered via a novelty pump that blows bags of the new Honey Sriracha-flavored Cheez-Its into their window. They can also purchase limited-edition Cheez-It graphic merchandise and nostalgic collectible items. I'm up for a $15K raise after the New Year—a bunch of salary space got freed up after KBM axed their DEI department.

I finally confronted Krauss the other day about his nephew interviewing for a position at KBM, hinting that nepotism might taint the integrity of the agency. He said he didn't have a nephew and had no clue what I was talking about. I haven't returned to the office since then.

My dermatillomania is the worst it's ever been. The urge to pick my cuticles is at a level that I can no longer control, like breathing or blinking. Washing my raw skin triggers an unbearable burning sensation, which somehow feels deserved. On any given day, four to seven of my fingers look mangled, like I've been in a fight with a small, aggressive animal. I started worrying about infections when the edges around one cut turned a faint gray, so I started carrying around this antibiotic ointment that smells like hospitals and Purell. Seeing new sores among my semi-healed wounds makes me feel ashamed, so I usually keep my hands in my pockets when I'm in public so people don't stare at them.

Last week, I ran out of Band-Aids and had to buy a new family-sized box at CVS. While waiting at the checkout counter, I looked at the covers of tabloid magazines. One headline was about a 93-year-old actor who was caught on camera groping the maître d' at a steakhouse in Manhattan. Another was about a TV hostess who got a breast reduction that went horribly wrong and nearly died from a skin infection. I also purchased a family-sized bag of Sour Patch Kids and ate all of them ravenously on the way home, nearly rear-ending a Honda Odyssey with a "Baby on Board" sticker.

Last week at the pool, I met a six-foot-tall Russian actress whose body was almost entirely covered in tattoos. She was wearing a black bikini that said "FATHER" across the left boob, "SON" across the right boob, and "HOLY SPIRIT" across her waxed crotch in silver sequins. I told her I was a novelist, which seemed to impress her, and when she asked what books I've written, I said "Nothing you'd like." We did anal in my shower, but I couldn't come so she left and I haven't seen or talked to her since then.

I'm trying to be a more informed citizen, so I've been consuming a steady diet of news from both sides of the political aisle to avoid trapping myself in any echo chambers. The one thing that everyone seems to agree on is that a nuclear war between the United States and Iran is inevitable. Meanwhile, the homeless population in Los Angeles is soaring to record highs. Tattered blue tents line the streets everywhere I go, and the people who live in them, rendered incoherent by fentanyl and pocked with needle wounds, wander aimlessly through intersections like zombies, babbling incoherently and gyrating uncontrollably. Conservatives are confident this is the inevitable result of lenient policies; liberals are confident this is the inevitable result of insufficient funding and resources. Last week, at a stoplight on my way to return a pair of Oliver Cabell Chelsea boots at Nordstrom, I watched a one-legged beggar wearing nothing but a Winnie-the-Pooh blanket defecate violently into a trash can on Fairfax in front of a woman and her two young daughters. They didn't seem to be fazed.

Suicides in the United States have reached an all-time high with more than 50,000 people offing themselves last year, according to the latest report from the CDC. A Canadian startup behind a 3D-printed pod that carries out assisted suicide is making its debut in America as early as next year. Teenagers in particular are taking their own lives at breakneck speed—I read a story in the *Los Angeles Times* about an elite prep school in Calabasas where four kids shot themselves during the fall semester alone. Experts said this was tragic but not terribly surprising. A group of parents is calling to cancel the school year.

The one thing that seems to hold Los Angeles together is the entertainment industry, which is expected to generate more than $120 billion by the end of this year. Recently, a movie about two stray dogs that forge a friendship was released to great fanfare, grossing more than $30 million in its first week. A 17-year-old social media star was awarded a three-year, $60 million deal from an audio streaming conglomerate to host a podcast that "puts a modern twist on feminism." The most popular song this month is by a 20-year-old porn star who raps about showing up to a nightclub and rejecting a guy who wants to have sex with her. Sometimes I'll listen to it at the gym or in the car—it's actually not that bad if you play it enough times. Paramount Pictures acquired the film rights to

Feral Symphony for $2.5 million in a fierce bidding war, with Martin DuVall serving as an Executive Producer.

I'm in the process of overhauling my personal care routine, starting with oral care. I switched to a fluoride-free hydroxyapatite toothpaste, but the consistency was runny and left a weird aftertaste in my mouth, so I threw it away and I'm on the hunt for a replacement. I also started using a bamboo water flosser. I swapped my antiperspirant for an aluminum-free deodorant because a meta-analysis found a strong correlation between aluminum salt exposure and Alzheimer's disease, several types of cancers, and reduced sperm count. I reduced my hair washing frequency to once every ten days because a dermatologist on Instagram told me the surfactants strip away the natural oils, even though I bought a $400 shower filter to get rid of chlorine. On the days I do wash my hair, I use a sulfate-free thickening shampoo infused with saw palmetto to stimulate my hair follicles. Lastly, I added a greens powder into my daily supplement routine after reading an interview in *Vogue* with a nutritionist who warned that the standard American diet under-delivers an adequate amount of vegetables, which are crucial for promoting healthy gut bacteria, providing essential minerals, and reducing oxidative stress. I'm thinking about doing a five-day water-only fast.

Someone at tempus told me that Sophia had a one-night stand with a 34-year-old pharmaceutical sales representative named Jeremy in Studio City. I spent an hour and a half sleuthing on Instagram until I found him. He moonlights as a DJ and his stage name is WØLF (stylized as "flow" backward). I haven't spoken to Duncan since we had lunch at the Chinese restaurant back in September. The word count of my novel has been sitting at 332 for more than a month.

Shrink

I'M AT A STANDOFF with Dr. Alper since he's been staring at me with this nonplussed look on his face for the past two minutes. He wants to know why I refuse to work on my novel after I told him how important it was to me. I said that's what I was paying him to figure out.

I tilt my head and try to see the ocean out the window, but there's too much smog. All I can make out are the hazy outlines of a few towers and a billboard that says "Hot Girls Have IBS." Using my right middle finger, I pry repeatedly at the inside of my thumb, but the pain is simply too excruciating. I override my instincts and place my hands on the armrests, but I'm worried Dr. Alper will notice the wounds, so I fold my arms across my chest. It suddenly feels really cold in here.

"Have you been taking your Effexor?" he finally asks.

"You're a useless fucking quack," I say with a cool indifference.

For a split second, his eyes widen. I can see his Adam's apple bob as he gulps—a primal reaction to my aggression. But then a coolness washes over his wizened face. The mind of the shrink kicks in.

"You have a right to be frustrated," he says, shakily. "But I won't have my medical expertise undermined."

I stand up slowly, casually stretch my arms above my head, and sidestep between the coffee table and my giant swivel chair before strolling out the door, closing it gently behind me. On the way home, I play the new Future album and turn the volume up really loud so I can't hear anything outside. Some old hag in a Lexus gives me a nasty look, but I just smile like a psychopath because I can tell it annoys her.

Palm Springs with Skylar

THIS WEEK CAN ONLY BE DESCRIBED as draining—physically, mentally, and emotionally. There's some problem with the Porsche's transmission temperature sensor, so I had to take it to the dealer, but they didn't have any loaners available, so I've been taking Uber Blacks to and from the office. At work yesterday, midway through an omakase lunch at Sasabune, Brooke told me that she's leaving KBM and moving back to Dallas because her sister was diagnosed with lymphoma and also because she wants to pivot to working in the nonprofit sector to "find more purpose." She's causing significant disruptions to the agency's workflow.

This morning, my maid sent me a text saying she was in the hospital because her appendix burst. The timing was brutal because I hosted a 20-year-old model I met on Raya at my apartment for dinner last night, had Uovo delivered via Postmates, and there's dried Arrabbiata sauce on my dining table. On top of all this, I have a case of mild plantar fasciitis flaring up in my right foot, which is preventing me from doing the kind of intense exercise I need to combat stress and keep an even keel.

I needed a quick getaway before the holidays, so I burned a few days of PTO (the HR department usually turns a blind eye, so it was really just a formality) and decided to drive out to my aunt Catherine's house in Palm Springs with my new fuck buddy, Skylar. I met her at a fundraising event last week that had something to do with the environment. Skylar is a 24-year-old Executive Assistant at a second-tier talent agency, coincidentally located across the street from my office. Her goal is to become a partner at the agency and elevate voices that would otherwise be overlooked in the entertainment industry. She also models and "creates content" for cosmetic companies.

Skylar is either Chinese or Korean. She's a little coy, but makes up for it with a dark sense of humor, which is what initially drew me to her (she said "this lobster roll tastes worse than the rat stew my grandparents survived on under communism").

Skylar is what I'd categorize as cute—not hot or beautiful. She has tired brown eyes that remind me of the color of Macallan 18, deep dimples, and jet-black hair cut in a mini bob that she's always pushing behind her ears. Yesterday, she asked when I got out of my last relationship—I lied and said nine months ago. I don't feel bad about bullshitting Skylar since I'm planning to ghost her once we get back to LA in a few days. We don't have anything in common (besides expensive taste and wanting to give each other earth-shattering orgasms), but I don't think that should preclude us from enjoying each other's company. I find deep comfort in impossibility, in the safety of a dead-end fling.

During the two-and-a-half-hour drive, we talked about romantic things: the best spots to watch sunsets in LA, the best type of cocoa for chocolate truffles, the best songs to have sex to (hers is "Partition" by Beyoncé, mine is "Lost Without U" by Robin Thicke). We rolled the windows down and played deep cuts by Frank Ocean and Outkast and Justin Timberlake. Sometimes, I even sang along when I remembered the lyrics. Somewhere near the exit for Beaumont, in the middle of a conversation about what I do to maintain my abs year-round,

Skylar unzipped my pants and started giving me the sloppiest road head I've gotten since high school. She put in a hero's effort, but I was paranoid and couldn't enjoy it because there was a convertible in front of us that kept veering into the right lane and jerking back into the fast lane. I assured her that we'd pick up where we left off once we got to the house, and she giggled, wiping a stream of saliva from her chin.

My aunt's house is in Vistas Las Palmas, an enclave of mid-century-modern gems in the shadow of Mount San Jacinto. The neighborhood includes homes once owned by Debbie Reynolds and Dean Martin. It was designed and built in 1962 by an architect who eventually died of a heroin overdose.

She commissioned a full renovation of the home in 2021, which took more than a year to finish, beginning with the exterior, where 35 barrel cacti were removed to make space for an outdoor dining and entertainment area. The backyard is lined with 20 olive trees, two oversized Bismarckia trees, and a lone Hercules aloe tree. Next to the jacuzzi, there's a marble bar and cooking station, refrigerated cabinets, a grill with a side burner, a pizza oven, and a retractable projection screen. Cathleen was adamant about avoiding the cliché lime green, bright orange, and yellow design features that are found throughout Palm Springs. Instead, she focused on more subtle features, like the original Wausau Tile that covers each room of the house. This was done to make the property feel more expansive, and also keep it cool in the summer heat. She opted to keep the low-slung lines of the home and hired a construction team to open the kitchen and the side of the house, installing a larger slider to promote a relaxing indoor-outdoor feel.

A real point of contention was the original fireplace, which is rigid, rustic, and screams 70s. However, once she saw it juxtaposed against the high-gloss Terrazzo floors up against it, along with the white ceilings and a pop of color from the Mario Bellini chenille rust-colored couch, she realized it actually looked fresh. The dining room is defined by metal, with the standout piece being a 70s burlwood credenza with brass inlay. This inspired a vintage Mastercraft brass pedestal table, which is mirrored in the raw brass floor lamp with alternating bulbs by Blueprint. The color palette in the kitchen pays homage to the desert. There's white oak cabinetry, accented by black fixtures by Brizo.

Cathleen was torn between a reeded and fluted pattern for the bar (which is also white oak) and ultimately chose reeded because it was more true to the home's midcentury roots. The countertop is a thin-cut, taupe-colored Taj Mahal quartzite, which is stain-resistant and practically bulletproof. My favorite part of the house is the family room, which is wrapped with Kelly Wearstler Graffito wallpaper; the eclectic lines give the space a new-wave vibe.

There's a navy blue Togo sofa by Ligne Roset and a Malayer rug that's supposedly 100 years old. Rounding out the space is a VPI Classic Signature turntable with Rogers custom amps and Klipsch Heresy speakers that were built in 1958. In the master bedroom, the star of the show is a custom-made mustard mohair bed, framed by geometric oxblood and nude-colored wallpaper, which was hand-painted. The master bathroom has an antique marble sink made from Bedrosian Stone and a 1,000-pound freestanding tub from Avalon 62, which required a crane for installation.

During our five days together in Palm Springs, I made a deliberate effort to initiate romantic activities with Skylar— things that Sophia probably deserved and expected, but I was too resentful to give her—convincing myself that they would lift me out of my rut and help me feel something besides disgust and apathy.

In the mornings, I'd make her breakfast in bed, which usually consisted of truffle omelets, assorted seasonal fruits, espressos served in vintage cups, and an occasional pastry, before snuggling beneath silk sheets, which usually led to sex. One morning, I surprised her with a bouquet of fresh roses and left a note in her Saint Laurent shopping bag that said "Just Because You're Cute, xx." After easing into the morning, we'd do some light physical activity, whether bicycling or swimming laps or jogging or playing tennis (I let her beat me a couple of times).

In the evenings, we'd take turns making dinner, which became more elaborate and intentional each night. We made seared scallops with Meyer lemon butter and trout roe; lamb rib chops with chickpea puree and olive tapenade; braised short ribs with pea smash, burnt carrot, ginger jam, and roasted garlic; black angus sirloin with smoked cipollini onion, roasted double star delicata squash, and bone broth reduction; Hawaiian Uku snapper with roasted okra and smoked tomato jam; diver scallops with chili garlic, spoon bread, and ginger scallion sauce; lemon and poppyseed sable with marcoot jersey quark mousse and peach compote; strawberry semifreddo with caramelized white chocolate crumb. We drank oxygenated mineral water and organic mezcal and well-aged bottles of Domaine Pontifical Châteauneuf du Pape.

While waiting for our meals to digest, I'd read Skylar passages from novels I haven't read, like *Sentimental Education* by Gustave Flaubert and *The Corrections* by Jonathan Franzen, and regurgitate reviews from Goodreads about why those passages were important.

One night, when I was just drunk enough, I told her that I dreamed of being a writer someday. I told her I believed, deep down, that writing was my singular path to fulfillment and self-actualization. I came clean about how desperate I was to distance myself from my family's sterile legacy and forge a new identity. I told her that being an Executive Creative Director makes me feel more worthless than any of the fentanyl addicts wasting away in tents under the freeways. I told her about my two meetings with Duncan and how he made me realize that I haven't experienced enough pain or struggle or loss in my life to have a real point of view. I told her that I wrote a letter to my parents requesting to be removed from my family's trust, but didn't have the balls to send it or even save the file on my computer. I told her that, despite all of this, I still had a novel in the works. I tried articulating the few disjointed plot lines and incomplete character arcs that I'd told countless people months ago. I knew I was rambling, but I couldn't stop myself. For the first time in my adult life, I really opened up. Skylar didn't seem impressed or even interested in my monologue—actually she seemed disturbed.

"Yeah, I guess everyone has a book in them," she said, before I excused myself to vomit in the bathroom.

At night, we listened to records on the VPI turntable, mostly Chet Baker's *Stairway to the Stars* and Bill Evans' *Portrait in Jazz*. We took bubble baths and gave each other massages with essential oils. We had heated, passionate, carnal sex on every piece of furniture in every room and nearly knocked over an abstract sculpture worth $17,000. We sipped Dom Ruinart champagne in the jacuzzi while the sun set behind us. We watched movies on the projector, our favorite being *Blue Velvet*, which we watched twice. Later, once the sky was black and the stars were out, we'd go skinny-dipping in the pool and run back into the house, covered in goosebumps, and make hot cocoa while shivering under fluffy white beach towels. Before bed, if we felt particularly glutinous, we'd indulge in treats like caramel toffee gelato and chocolate chunk cookies with flaky sea salt, and we'd convince ourselves it was fine because life's short and we'd get our 10K steps in the next day.

On our last night together, we fell asleep naked on the couch, wasted on Bordeaux and a bottle of $250 scotch that I had delivered to the house via Postmates. I woke up at 6 a.m. on the dot and remembered it was the last Tuesday of the month, so I checked my Citigold Private Client Checking Account app and the $45,000 deposit from my trust was there, like always. I climbed over Skylar, making sure not to wake her, walked outside into the pitch black, and ripped at the cuticles on my right thumb until the sun rose from behind the San Jacinto Mountains.

ACKNOWLEDGEMENTS

Thank you...

To Danny, for the title and red ink

To Matilda, for trying

To Vivian, for the cover idea

To Catie, for the cover art

To Leah, for the fit checks

To LA, for the material

Dominic Vaiana is a ghostwriter and the author of *A Bar in Toledo: The Untold Story of a Mafia Front Man and a Grammy-Winning Song*. He lives in Los Angeles. *Gray Sleep* is his first novel.